W9-CAB-617

BRAVELANDS

OATHKEEPER

BRAVELANDS

BRAVELANDS

OATHKEEPER

ERIN
HUNTER

HARPER
An Imprint of HarperCollins*Publishers*

Library of Congress Cataloging-in-Publication Data

Names: Hunter, Erin, author.
Title: Oathkeeper / Erin Hunter.
Description: First edition. | New York : Harper, an imprint of HarperCollinsPublishers, [2020]
| Series: Bravelands ; [#6] | Audience: Ages 8-12. | Audience: Grades 4-6. | Summary: "With
the balance of Bravelands at a breaking point, the Great Herd must risk everything to unite
against their common enemy: the rogue lion, Titan"— Provided by publisher.
Identifiers: LCCN 2020008884 | ISBN 978-0-06-264222-6 (hardcover) | ISBN 978-0-06-
264223-3 (library binding)
Subjects: CYAC: Baboons—Fiction. | Lion—Fiction. | Elephants—Fiction. | Adventure and
adventurers—Fiction. | Africa—Fiction.
Classification: LCC PZ7.H916625 Oat 2020 | DDC [Fic]—dc23
LC record available at https://lccn.loc.gov/2020008884

Typography by Ellice M. Lee
20 21 22 23 24   PC/LSCH   10 9 8 7 6 5 4 3 2 1
❖
First Edition

BRAVELANDS

OATHKEEPER

PROLOGUE

A few years earlier . . .

The sun blazed high and white over Bravelands, steeping the whole savannah in a dazzling paleness. Rivers glittered like thin streaks of silver far below, and the forests were smudges of green. Highcrest's piercing gaze made out her own shadow, flickering across the golden grasslands; a couple of giraffes tilted up their horned heads to watch the great crowned eagle pass overhead. Their ears swiveled and flicked; then, unthreatened, they returned to browsing on tall acacias.

Highcrest's eyes moved on, searching, always searching. Her chicks were hungry, their beaks forever gaping for more food, and she had hunted too long already. The need for prey warred inside her with the urgency to return to the nest, to protect them from daring predators.

There! Something moved on the grassland far below, a flickering shadow of darker gold, something that bolted heedlessly across the open plain. Perhaps it was fleeing some flesh-eater, but it was too foolish, or too panicked, to glance skyward for a different danger. Highcrest adjusted her wings, stooping through the air to follow the creature's path.

It was a lion cub, she could see now. It stumbled every few pawsteps, but picked itself up and fled again, as if a pack of jackals were on its stubby tail. Highcrest could see no predators in pursuit—the cub must have lost them some time ago, if they ever existed—yet still it hurtled on, clearly terrified.

Highcrest felt no pity for the exhausted little lion. Far from here, her own offspring waited for her, beaks open, bellies empty. This lost and frightened cub, prideless and motherless, would be an easy kill.

Easier, in fact, than even she had thought. As she cocked her head and swooped lower, the small lion stumbled again. This time it could not regain its footing and tripped headlong over its forepaws, crashing hard to the dry earth.

Silent, Highcrest angled her wings and dived. The cub lay immobile—it must have struck its fragile skull on one of the scattered rocks; perhaps it was dead already. Truly, the Great Spirit looked kindly on Highcrest and her chicks today!

Highcrest plummeted and sank her extended talons into the cub's limp flanks. Through her claws she could feel the weak thrum of blood within it; it was still alive, then, but there was nothing it could do now. With strong beats of her broad wings, she took to the skies again, the cub gripped in her talons.

The prey was heavier than her usual hares and hyraxes,

but Highcrest was determined to hang on to this Spirit-given bounty. Although her wing muscles ached, she flew on grimly, rising as steeply as she could into the high currents of air. By the time her nest came in sight, balanced on a high kigelia branch in a clump of woodland, she was exhausted but exhilarated.

A little awkwardly, she flapped down, dropping her burden with a thump onto the tangle of wood. Instantly the chicks were alert and excited, eyes bright and beaks wide, their squeals of hunger high-pitched. Yet Highcrest could not help herself—she took a moment to call to her mate, desperate to show him their prize. Flexing her sore wings, she hopped a little way along the branch, letting out a triumphant screech to call him back to the nest. This food would not only satisfy their chicks; it would last the grown birds for days.

Behind her, near where the branch met the tree's sturdy trunk, something rustled. Sharply, Highcrest jerked her head around.

The cub was moving. It blinked and swayed, hauling itself onto its forepaws, mewling weakly.

She could not risk it falling, perhaps to be snatched by some other predator. Highcrest hopped back along the branch, opening her powerful curved beak to tear at its neck, to put an end to its pitiful struggles.

And then a face burst through the foliage: a long-snouted, bright-eyed, intelligent face. Its amber eyes glittered as they met Highcrest's.

Baboon! With a shrill cry of anger, Highcrest spread her

wings to their fullest extent, her shadow looming over the baboon. The creature did not even flinch. Peeling back its lips to expose its long yellow fangs, it gave a screech of mocking defiance. Then, right under her broad wings, it sprang forward and snatched up the lion cub by the scruff of the neck.

The baboon was gone before Highcrest's lunge reached it; her beak raked at nothing but twigs and foliage. With a scream of frustration, she flapped her wings, but the only sign of the baboon was a few dislodged dry leaves that rattled down toward the earth far below.

The prey was gone; the hunt must begin again. There was no point in rage or regret.

So much for the Great Spirit's favor!

CHAPTER ONE

Damp trails of gray smoke curled into the blue sky and drifted across the grassland to dissipate into the heat haze. The forest, once so lush and green, was a broken and blackened waste of mud and ruined stumps. The sudden rain had passed, leaving an acrid reek.

Fearless stood very still, his head high, the tip of his tail twitching. Behind him, his new pride waited in silence; he could feel their presence without having to turn, as if their force flowed into him.

And he needed that silent strength. Before him stood the black-maned brute everyone had said was dead. Fearless had never believed it, of course. He had known this creature still lived—sensed it in his blood—a malevolent presence lingering in Bravelands. The beast who had killed his father, Loyal; the murderer who had tricked his adoptive father, Gallant; the savage who had watched in approval as his mother, Swift, was blinded.

Titan. The lion I have sworn to kill.

Those black, mad eyes met his, and Fearless's body shook with hatred. He did not look away.

Behind Titan, too, stood a supportive pride, but these were not lions. Hackles high, sharp small teeth bared, yellow eyes glowing with malice, they were the golden wolves who had spread blood and havoc across Bravelands for the last few moons. As they prowled and paced, they had the powerful elegance of lions, and Fearless knew the reason: that aura they had was stolen from the lions they had killed, the ones whose spirits they had consumed.

Titan's soft, menacing growl broke the silence. "You've grown, Fearless."

"Yes." Fearless's voice was stronger and clearer than he'd worried it would be. "Grown enough to fulfill my oath, Titan. I was only a cub when I swore to kill you, but I mean to keep my promise." He tightened his shoulders and bared his teeth. "I challenge you, murderer. Fight me. Here and now."

Before he had taken two paces toward Titan, he heard the in-drawn breaths of his pride.

"Wait!" gasped Ruthless.

A small figure dashed to Titan's side: Menace, his brattish cub and Ruthless's own sister. She drew back her muzzle in a contemptuous sneer, revealing her small, sharp fangs.

"Let me kill him for you, Father."

Titan glanced down at her, his eyes burning with delight.

"Truly, you are my cub, Menace. But this fight is not for you. Back!"

"Yes, back," snarled Fearless, glaring at the cub who had once been under his protection. She had always been arrogant and self-serving, but there was a new cruelty about her now, and he had no time for her. "No more games!"

"Ha!" Titan's fangs gleamed yellow, dripping with slaver. "Indeed, Fearless: no more games. You would be wise to turn and flee. Run away, like the terrified cub you were when I killed Gallant. You are still that cub, however much you posture and snarl. Fearless, the ill-named coward who has no place in Bravelands!" Titan's eyes gleamed with madness. "You think you can defeat me *now*? When I am stronger than I have ever been? My heart and belly are filled with the spirits of those I've killed. Their strength is mine. Run and hide again with baboons. You have less chance against me now than you did then!"

Fearless growled, deep in his throat. "Make your speeches, Titan. They won't help you." He paced deliberately forward.

"Well, if you insist." Titan hunched his powerful shoulders. "I'll take your heart as I took the heart of the Great Parent."

One paw still raised, he felt it tremble. *Thorn? What?*

"That's right," growled Titan. "That baboon who claimed to lead all of Bravelands? A tasty heart, so full of spirit."

Fearless's throat felt dry and tight, and his belly twisted. Thorn was dead? The baboon who had been his friend and ally and confidant his whole life?

It can't be true—

Yet he knew from Titan's evil snarl that the brute was not lying. Rage and grief burned in his gut, and he broke into a sudden charge, streaking across the plain to bury his claws in Titan's neck.

Sleek yellow shapes darted immediately to their black-maned leader, surrounding and guarding him, their skinny paws kicking up dust that rose in clouds. Fearless's throat burned and his eyes stung, and for a moment his paws faltered, but he ran grimly on. He felt sharp fangs sink into his shoulder and right flank, but he shook the wolves away, swiping one aside with a powerful paw. It yelped and tumbled into the dust, but more took its place, biting and clawing.

In the chaos, dust rose and swirled, obscuring Fearless's vision. Furious, he growled and struck out, dislodging more wolves. Through the gloom drifted Titan's vicious taunts.

"You couldn't save any of them, could you, Fearless? Not your father, not your dear friend Loyal. Not your mother. You couldn't even save that baboon!"

Follow his voice, thought Fearless. *Lucky that he can't resist talking.* With a savage blow he struck away another wolf and bounded toward the sound of Titan's taunts. Off to his left something was happening, the yelps and frightened growls of a smaller lion under attack from the wolves—but he couldn't afford to lose his focus. The others of his pride could deal with that. Fearless was so close to Titan now; the brute's outline loomed in the murk, and Fearless coiled his haunches to launch his attack.

Menace sprang out of the dust clouds to block his way. Her eyes glittered.

"Attack my father? Or save Useless?"

Fearless scrabbled to a halt, shocked.

He heard an amused growl from Titan. "An unnecessary game, my cub, but a fun one. Let's see what he does, shall we? Choose wisely, Fearless."

Menace swung her small head to yelp at a group of wolves. "Kill him! Kill my traitor of a brother!"

For a moment Fearless stood in agonized indecision, staring. That commotion he'd seen from the corner of his eye: two wolves had separated young Ruthless from the pride and were dragging him to a bare patch of ground, their teeth in his leg and side. His eyes rolled wildly with terror.

"Titan! Call them off!" roared Fearless. "Even you wouldn't kill your own cub!"

"Ruthless is no longer my cub," growled Titan, pacing forward. "He sided with my enemy. My spirit-pride may do as they please with him."

Menace smirked at Fearless in vicious triumph. Howling with delight, more wolves fell on the cowering Ruthless. Fearless could hear his pride behind him, roaring with fury as they leaped forward. But he was the closest to Ruthless, and he knew he had no choice; he twisted away from Titan and sprang at the wolves.

Snapping, tearing, and clawing, Fearless could only channel his frustration into his attack on the golden wolves. He felt his fangs rip into warm flesh, his paws slam against skulls and spines, and one by one the wolves tumbled away, yelping and whimpering. Through his fog of blood-rage, Fearless became aware of the rest of his pride, joining him to attack the wolves without mercy.

Now the fight was truly unequal, and it was only moments before the surviving wolves turned tail and fled, leaving a battered and bloodied Ruthless panting on the ground. Yet when Fearless spun back toward Titan, the black-maned brute and his daughter had disappeared.

Fearless bounded toward the place where Titan had stood. There was nothing there but pawprints, yellow mangled grass, and the stench of evil.

Throwing back his head, he gave a roar of fury.

"You'll face me, you coward. One day, you'll face me!"

And on that day, Titan, you'll die.

CHAPTER TWO

Sky's trunk tingled with the reek of burned timber and vegetation. The beautiful forest was destroyed, the trunks nothing but charred skeletons, and the earth was blackened mud beneath her feet; yet Sky felt a deep, joyous hope. Her life-mate, Rock, stood at her shoulder, his body pressed against hers for support.

Bravelands will recover, she thought, closing her eyes to better sense Rock's warmth and the thrum of his heartbeat against her hide. *And so will Rock. He lives, and I love him. That's all that matters.* Gently she touched the tip of her trunk to one of the raw scars on his shoulder.

"Your wounds must hurt," she murmured.

"No," he said softly, leaning his head closer into hers. "Not badly. And they don't matter, now that we've found each other again. I've missed you, Sky, so very much."

"And I—" Something stirred between Sky's shoulder blades,

and she twisted her head to peer back at the tiny baboon that crouched there, half asleep. "Rock," she murmured, "I wish we could stay here together, for longer. But we must begin searching for a mother for this orphan. She needs one, and quickly, if she's to survive."

"We'll save her," Rock replied. "I think we owe that to the Great Spirit. But where will you find a nursing baboon who will take her? It's almost certain that this little one's mother is dead."

Sky's mind was already racing. Taking the baby to a rival troop would be risky—males had been known to kill offspring from other troops—but they needed to find a nursing mother.

"Female baboons are kind, I know that," she said, softly.

"Female elephants are kind, too," rumbled Rock, peering down at a fallen tree in amusement. "After all, you've looked after these little strangers since their mother died."

Nimble and Lively, the two young cheetahs, were not so little anymore, thought Sky as she watched them fondly. Their fluffy mantles had all but molted away, and they were growing long-legged and sleek. Yet they still nosed and pawed around the charred trunk like excited cubs. Sky thought they were playing a game, but then Nimble glanced up at Rock. "There's something trapped under here."

"Really?" Rock cocked his ears forward; one of them was badly torn where it had caught on a smoldering, jutting branch. "Let's have a look. Move aside a bit, Lively; I don't want to trample you."

Obediently, Lively backed away, her nostrils still flaring

with curiosity. Rock butted the tree hard with his upper trunk, and when Sky joined in to help, the two elephants at last dislodged the huge piece of timber from its resting place. It came suddenly loose and bumped and rocked to a halt a little way away.

Almost at once, shapes moved in a hollow beneath where the tree had lain. A long nose probed the air, drawing in a delighted breath. A slender head followed the exposed snout, and then an adult anteater emerged from the hidden cavity, followed by its young.

"Thank you!" she grunted, nodding eagerly to Sky and Rock. "We hid in our den from the fire, but this tree collapsed and blocked the entrance. We're grateful you came along."

"Thank the young cheetahs," said Rock. "They're the ones who found you."

The anteater nodded to the cubs, a little warily. "Thank you, then. It was terribly hot in there."

"The tree probably saved you from the fire, though," chirped Lively.

"True, true," agreed the anteater, and the whole family waddled away toward the savannah, noses snuffling the breeze. "Come along, pups. We'll find some tasty termites and you'll feel much better. . . ."

The anteater's voice faded as the elephants and the young cheetahs watched them go. Sky smiled and nudged Rock.

"You see? There's hope."

"Sometimes," he agreed. "The forest will live again, too. This has happened before; I remember the older bulls telling us about fires. They're terrible things, but they can't ever destroy Bravelands completely."

"Rock's right!" mewed Nimble, rising onto his hind paws and peering upward. "Look, there are birds coming back already." He batted a paw half-heartedly, as if he might swipe one of the blue starlings from the sky.

"And soon the vultures will come, too, and clear the dead," Sky added. She lowered her head sadly, thinking of the animals that had died so horribly. But life and death were the way of Bravelands, and Rock was right: the forest would send out green shoots and grow back to its old lush glory.

Life and death are the way of Bravelands . . . and terrible things happened every day, with no warning, no mercy. Sky turned abruptly to Rock. "I'm sorry," she told him.

"For what?" He looked surprised.

"I'm sorry for ever believing you were capable of killing River." Sky pressed her head against his shoulder, twining her trunk with his.

"Don't mention it again, Sky," he murmured. "I don't blame you for thinking it. I barely knew myself what had happened."

"No. I should have known all along, even before I read her bones, that it was an accident. I knew you better than that, Rock, and I should have trusted my instincts, trusted *you*." She raised her eyes to his. "Please forgive me for that lack of faith."

"How can I not?" Rock looked startled. "Sky, I still haven't quite forgiven myself. The Rage is a dreadful thing, but we bulls cannot shirk all responsibility for what happens while we're in its grip. We must accept that we lose ourselves, lose control of our strength, and feel the remorse for what we might have done."

"Acceptance and regret, perhaps," she agreed sternly, "but not guilt, Rock. It's time to let that go. River's death is in the past, and all of us have paid for it—you, Boulder, and me too. Let her rest in peace now."

Rock nodded somberly. "You're wise, Sky. And kind."

"And we can be together at last, without guilt," she added. "Nothing stands in our way anymore. Nothing, except . . ."

"What?" He blinked at her.

She sighed and drew back a little, though her trunk remained twined with his. "I don't carry the Great Spirit anymore, Rock, but I still feel a closeness to it—a responsibility for it, and for Bravelands. I can't abandon the Spirit, and I can't simply walk away to my own happiness. Bravelands is still under threat, from these evil spirit-eaters. If Bravelands has no peace from them, we never truly will either."

Sky felt her muscles stiffen with resolve as Rock nodded, and she lifted her head a little higher.

"I have to help the Great Parent defeat the threat the wolves pose," she said firmly.

"And so do I, Sky. We're life-mates, and I'll be at your side come what may." Rock's voice was steady as he gazed at her.

Warmth rushed through her body. Closing her eyes, Sky pressed her head to his. Despite his wounds she could feel his indomitable strength, and it gave her hope. They would all need determination like Rock's, she suspected, in the battles to come.

"We should go and find our herds," she whispered. "There is so much work to do."

Together the two young elephants trudged through the churned black earth of the ruined forest, leaving the odors of death and smoke behind to head for the open savannah and its clear air. Nimble and Lively trotted happily alongside them, and Sky could feel the baboon stirring as they walked. She raised her trunk-tip to touch the baby with gentle reassurance.

It was so good to feel unburned grass and earth beneath her feet, and to smell the fragrant warm air that was free of ash. Sky paused for a moment, to drink it all in and to scan the savannah. There, in the middle distance on the shimmering plain, milled the mass of elephants who had heeded her call to help the Great Parent fight the flames: the bull herds and the female herds, all intermingled.

Some of the elephants turned as Sky and Rock ambled closer, and more than a few ears flapped in astonishment. A trumpet of greeting rang out: it was Comet's voice, Sky realized, the matriarch of her own family. Star and old Flint were right behind her. Yet some of the other elephants continued to shoot Rock suspicious glances, especially the females of Mahogany Marcher's herd. They grumbled quietly, even though Mahogany herself strode forward to greet Rock and Sky.

"Mahogany." Rock stepped forward before a word could be said and lowered his head humbly. "I owe you an apology that I've never had a chance to give."

"Rock." The old matriarch nodded thoughtfully. "I am glad to see you alive. The past is the past, young bull, and River herself would want us all to put this behind us."

Sky pressed close to Rock again, feeling his muscles sag with relief beneath his dark hide. "Rock and I," she told Mahogany, and drew a breath, "we'd like to renew our pledge to each other."

"And I'm happy to hear it," said Mahogany, stroking Sky's ear with her trunk. "Let *all* hear it, Sky Strider."

Swallowing, Sky nodded and raised her head. Her eyes swept the watching herds, her heart thudding in her chest.

"Rock and I are life-mates once more," she cried, loudly and clearly. "In the sight of the Great Spirit, now and forever."

The elephants again exchanged rapid murmurs, and though there were still a few doubtful rumbles and querulous cries, those were soon drowned out by the trumpets of happiness and congratulation. One by one the elephants moved toward Sky and Rock, their greeting calls swelling in volume.

One young bull broke free of his herd and came trotting forward, his eyes solemn. Sky recognized her brother Boulder, the bull who had battled Rock in the fatal duel for River's affections. He knew the truth about River's death; she had explained it to him. But Sky was not at all sure how he would react to this news of their pledge-renewal; it was he and his herd-brothers who had driven out Rock in the first place.

Boulder halted before her, blowing at the dust. He nodded to her, then turned to Rock.

"Rock," he rumbled, "my brother bull. I have spoken to my herd and we would like to welcome you once more, if it is your wish to join us."

"Boulder." Rock's voice brimmed with relief and happiness. "I'm glad to."

Boulder dipped his head, then raised it to let his voice carry loud and clear. "And if Sky chooses you as her life-mate, Rock, I respect her decision. More than that—I am happy for you both. All the herds should respect both your choices."

"Thank you, Boulder," Sky murmured, her throat tight with emotion.

All the elephants were surging closer now, stretching out their trunks toward Rock and Sky. Rock's herd gathered around him, their great ears flapping. Sky felt the touch of a trunk-tip on her shoulder: Comet's.

"Sky, I'm so pleased for you."

"That means a lot, Comet." Sky butted her matriarch's shoulder fondly.

"The herds plan to remain together for a few days," Comet went on. "It's unusual, but then these times are strange. Why end it all before we are ready? But soon"—she paused, looking deep into Sky's eyes—"soon we must go our separate ways."

Sky knew what Comet was saying. The times were strange indeed, but the old practices could not be abandoned. It had been such a long time since she had traveled with the female herd, as was right and proper. . . .

"I know we must." Sky nodded thoughtfully. "And Comet, I'm ready at last to rejoin the Strider herd. I will be with you, I promise. But this little baboon needs a mother." She curled up her trunk to stroke the vulnerable creature between her shoulder blades, and it crooned in sleepy contentment. "It's my responsibility to find it one."

Comet laughed softly. "I understand, Sky. It's your way, and I would never want you to change. Nor would any elephant in Bravelands—or any creature. In some ways you're like the mother to us all."

Sky felt embarrassment and pleasure all at once. *One day I will travel with the female herd again. I know it. But not quite yet . . .*

"Good-bye, Comet," she whispered, pressing her head to her matriarch's. "I'll see you again very soon, I hope."

Sky turned, raising her trunk in farewell to her own herd and the others. Rock drew away from his brother bulls and trudged to her side.

He laid his trunk across hers.

"We have more time together, Sky. Let's share our good fortune and find this little baboon a family."

Sky cast frequent glances back as they went on their way, watching the herds of her kind until their forms were rippling smudges in the heat haze, and then lost completely in the horizon. They crossed a small river that lapped up to her knees, and the small baboon took a little water from her trunk. As they climbed the bank on the far side, Rock halted just ahead.

"Wait, Sky."

She came to a stop beside him. His ears flapped forward, and both elephants scanned the broad sweep of the savannah before them. Heat made the grassland shimmer, and the acacia trees on the plain seemed to tremble. Far in the distance, herds of zebras and antelope moved, leisurely grazing; but closer to Rock and Sky, something else shifted in the bright sunlight: tawny shapes that were indistinct smears of gold in the camouflaging grass.

"Lions," murmured Sky, "and they're coming our way."

"It's a big pride." Rock narrowed his green eyes, and she felt him tense. "Perhaps we should avoid them. Ordinarily I'd be sure they wouldn't attack, but these days, who can be certain of anything?"

"No." Sky peered harder into the shimmer of heat. "Rock, I recognize some of them. Look, that pale one is Honor, and next to her is Resolute. They're Titanpride lions!"

Agitated, Rock made a deep rumble in his throat. "Then we'll take a route that skirts them."

But as they did so, the lions changed course too, clearly intending to intercept. Sky's heart clenched, but any fear quickly gave way to anger. If Titan's band wanted to try something foolhardy, she was confident that she and Rock between them would see it off. She was about to trumpet a warning at the approaching pride when her heart gave a leap of recognition. "Hold on, that's Fearless! He's leading them!"

"Fearless?" asked Rock, his ears flapping out defensively. "With Titanpride?"

"But I don't see Titan." Sky felt a shiver of uncertainty beneath her hide. "It doesn't make sense. Fearless leads Titanpride lions? Something's happened, and I need to know what. Fearless won't hurt me, Rock, I'm certain of that. I have to speak with him."

Rock took a deep breath, then blew it out heavily through his trunk. "I'll be watching their every move."

As the pride drew close enough for Sky to see Fearless's face very clearly, she narrowed her eyes. She was still unafraid of her old ally, but it was clear Fearless had grown and changed. His shoulders were broader, his legs strongly muscled. His whole presence was far bigger than she remembered. And a mane had grown quite swiftly since she had seen him last, already bushy enough to frame his fierce and determined face. Now he truly was a lion who could inspire fear.

Raising her trunk, Sky let out a solemn trumpet of greeting. Fearless's ears pricked, and he picked up his pace, bounding to meet her.

"Sky Strider," he greeted her formally, halting to lift his head high. "I thought it was you."

"Your pride—" she began.

"Many are Titan's former pride, yes." He nodded grimly. "They no longer follow that brute, Sky. We are Fearlesspride now."

Sky and Rock exchanged a nervous look of relief. "Then it's all the more good to see you, Fearless," she told the lion warmly.

Suddenly Fearless looked far less certain of himself, and as he licked his jaws in hesitation his gaze slid away from hers. "I'm glad to have met you here too, Sky, but sorry for the news I bring."

Sky narrowed her eyes, silent for a moment, and Fearless's eyes met hers once again. She frowned. His were dark with emotion—*Grief*, she thought suddenly, with a lurch in her chest.

"Fearless, what's happened?"

"Thorn," he began. "Great Father Thorn—"

But his voice seemed to catch in his throat, and he had to swallow hard and lick his jaws again before he could go on speaking. Sky's heart hammered with fear. "*What*, Fearless? Tell me!"

"He's dead. Sky, Thorn is dead." The young lion's voice was rough with anguish. "Titan found him and took his heart."

This time, it was Sky who couldn't speak. A huge surge of grief filled her throat, and she felt herself sway; the baby baboon slipped a little and Rock instantly shifted his body supportively against hers. She blinked hard.

"The Great Father is dead?" she stammered at last, hoarsely. "They killed him?" Slowly, agonizingly, the full meaning of Fearless's words began to penetrate the chaos in her mind. *They took his heart. They took the heart of the Great Parent!*

"No!" she cried, wildly jerking away from Rock and taking two rapid, stumbling steps forward. "The Great Spirit lived within Thorn!"

Fearless stared at her, a dawning horror in his eyes, as if the implications had only just struck him. "You mean . . ."

"Does Titan have the strength of the Great Spirit now?" Sky felt herself sway again, dizzied by horror. "Or is the Great Spirit *dead*?"

"If you're right, Sky," rumbled Rock as he drew close to her once more, "this is a disaster for more than just Thorn's friends. It's a catastrophe for all of Bravelands."

"I should have known!" trumpeted Sky, a dark despair

swamping her. "I should have sensed that the Spirit was in such danger. Why didn't I know?" *Perhaps*, a small voice whispered inside her, *because you were so wrapped up in finding Rock again, too obsessed with your own happiness. . . .*

"Sky, don't blame yourself!" Rock stroked her shoulder with his trunk. "You're not the one who killed him. Titan did that!"

"The wolves, led by Titan," snarled Fearless. "Thorn was my best friend, Sky. I understand your fears for the Great Spirit, but I can't think about that right now. It's Thorn I mourn, and it's Thorn I will avenge!"

"I know." Her voice broke. "I mourn him too, Fearless."

The lion's face grew tormented. "But before I even think of vengeance, I have to bring this news to his troop. I still have friends there—Thorn's friends. His mate, Berry. She has to know, and it will break her heart."

"We'll go together." Sky tried to draw herself up, though her muscles trembled with shock. "You, Rock, and I: we'll tell Dawntrees that Thorn is lost. And somehow . . ." She felt a wrench of grief and pity. "Somehow, we have to try to bring comfort to Berry. Though I fear that might not even be possible."

CHAPTER THREE

He could not stay away from the place where Berry's body lay. If he couldn't see her, it felt as if he was abandoning her. Already a faint odor of death was spreading through the shadowy glade. Thorn knew that insects and rot-eaters would come; perhaps some were here already. It was the way of Bravelands, though he couldn't bear to contemplate it.

But perhaps that death-odor was a trick; perhaps there was still hope? His breath rough in his throat, Thorn padded toward the mounded shape beside a scattering of small boulders.

Berry lay there still; she hadn't leaped up miraculously, she didn't turn to him with laughing eyes and tell him it had all been a trick, a joke. No: in the end she had played only one great trick, and that was to pretend to the wolves that she was the true Great Parent. Berry had sacrificed herself to Titan and his cohorts so that Thorn himself could go on living.

And I wish so much that she hadn't. It should have been me lying there.

Berry looked almost peaceful, and Thorn was glad her eyes were closed; he couldn't bear to see them sink back in her skull, their gleaming brightness dulled by death. As it looked now, she could have been sleeping. The wound in her chest was still concealed by the heaped flowers Mud had put there, as the little baboon tried desperately to hide her fate from Thorn.

The wolves had taken her heart, her spirit. Berry would never wait for Thorn now, in the silver forests by the River of Stars. She was gone, gone altogether. He would never see her again, not even in death.

There was the pad of paws and soft breathing behind him, but Thorn didn't jump or turn; his senses felt dull and blunt, as if he would never laugh or be happy—or even feel fear—ever again.

"Thorn," Mud murmured softly at his shoulder. "I'm sorry. I know you want to be here. But you can't stay. Please, Thorn, you have to flee. When Titan finds out—" The small baboon cleared his throat, staring at the corpse beneath the flowers. "When he finds out about Berry's deception, he'll be angrier than ever. Titan will come after you again with his wolf pack, and he'll hunt you down without mercy."

"I can't run," muttered Thorn, not taking his eyes off Berry. "If I flee now, Berry's sacrifice will have meant nothing. She did this for me and for Bravelands, and I won't let her down. There's no way I can abandon Bravelands to Titan and his madness. He's done so much damage already; his wolves have spilled so much blood. It can't go on." At last he turned to face Mud. "I can't *let* it go on."

Two more baboons approached on silent paws: Nut and Spider, both of them unusually solemn. Nut came closer to put a paw on Thorn's shoulder.

"Mud's right, Thorn," he said softly. "You can't face Titan down—not physically. You need time to think, to plan, to come up with a strategy." Nut sat back on his haunches, gazing steadily at Thorn. "Remember all we've learned since you became Great Father? So many animals were surprised at the Great Spirit's choice, but we know for sure now: being Great Parent isn't about physical strength. It's about wisdom and cleverness. You have plenty of both, so give yourself time to make use of them."

"It's true," Spider broke in, his eyes almost popping with eagerness. "It's not about strength, Thorn-friend. Spider knows it, because a pygmy mouse was Great Parent once. So clever he was! The pygmy mouse Great Parent was only teeny tiny, but he kept every Bravelands creature in order—lions, leopards, even buffalo!"

"And who did you hear this story from, Spider?" asked Nut, rolling his eyes. "Was it from a pygmy mouse, by any chance?"

"Yes, indeed!" Spider nodded. "That's how Spider knows it's true!"

Nut sighed, and Thorn couldn't help but feel a smile twitching at his muzzle.

"I'm sure Spider's story is true in its essence, Nut," he said quietly, "and that's what matters. Maybe you're all right: maybe

I should take a step back and think about things for a while. Maybe . . . maybe at the ravine. It's well hidden." He swallowed hard, thinking of the times he and Berry used to meet secretly there, when their love was still forbidden by their troop. He couldn't help but turn to her corpse again, his heart aching with the longing for her to leap up and laugh at him.

A branch above him creaked, and he glanced up. There sat Stinger, grinning down at him.

Thorn did not even flinch. *He isn't real*, he thought dully.

Extending a lazy paw, Stinger snatched up a brown scorpion that scuttled up the trunk. He snapped off its tail and began to chew on its body, his mocking eyes never leaving Thorn's.

"So you're going to run away, *Great Father*? Hmm?"

Thorn ignored him.

"Look at you! Is this what you thought your life would become?" Stinger tilted his head and grinned. "Take it from one who knows, Thorn: you won't feel better till you take your vengeance. Stop moping and take it! Do it *now*. For Berry's sake."

Thorn stared up at him. Those cool amber eyes glittered with mischief as Stinger sucked the meat from inside the scorpion.

"Don't you care enough? Didn't you love my daughter, Thorn? Look at her!"

A hand took hold of Thorn's arm, pulling him back to reality. "Try not to think about the body," Nut murmured. "That's not Berry, not really. It's only her pelt and her bones, and the rot-eaters will come for it soon, and she will become part of Bravelands. It's how it should be."

Her body will become part of Bravelands, thought Thorn. *Yes. But her spirit will never fly to the stars. It's been stolen, murdered as surely as her body was.*

Thorn glanced up, just to be sure the vision of Stinger had indeed gone. Still, though, the old baboon's words echoed in his mind. Was vengeance the answer? Easy to say, but almost impossible to achieve.

Mud exchanged a worried glance with Spider. "Thorn, if you're retreating to the ravine, let the three of us come with you."

"That's a good idea," agreed Nut.

"Thorn-friend needs us right now." Spider nodded.

Thorn bit on his lip. A clump of straggly lantana grew by the tree root beside him; he plucked a pawful of its tiny orange blooms and laid them carefully with the others on Berry's chest. Maybe it was his imagination, but the death-odor seemed stronger now; Bravelands was taking her. Shutting his eyes, he blew out a heavy breath.

"Mud should come with me," he told his friends, "but Nut and Spider, I want you to stay here. I don't know how Dawn-trees Troop will react to this; Berry was once their Crownleaf, after all. Would you keep an eye on them for me?"

Nut took a breath to argue; then, reluctantly, he nodded.

Thorn turned to Mud. "Come on, my old friend. Let's head for the ravine. I have so much to think about, and I need your advice more than ever."

CHAPTER FOUR

Fearless's heart was heavy as he padded toward the Great Father Clearing. His pride had held back, waiting at the borders of the trees, and the forest was unusually silent, the air heavy and hot. Although Sky and Rock paced as delicately as they could behind Fearless, their movement seemed astonishingly loud in the weighty peace of the forest. Barely the stir of an insect disturbed the quietness; no birds sang.

But as the trees thinned and the glade opened before him, Fearless caught sight of vultures circling in the blue circle of sky above. His gut wrenched. Already some of the huge birds had landed by the lifeless furred shape in the clearing and were tugging at strips of its flesh.

That was strange, thought Fearless. He remembered how the vultures had refused to touch the body of Great Mother, how they had guarded the murdered elephant themselves out of respect. Did that respect not extend to Thorn, the baboon Great Father?

Fearless swallowed hard and pushed though the last branches into the clearing. At once, some of the vultures scattered, glaring and cawing at him, but he ignored their flapping wings. He walked forward. The smell of death was strong, though the corpse was half-obscured by scattered flowers.

Something about the odor was wrong. Fearless frowned and flared his nostrils, tentatively drawing in the scent. Of course death changed creatures, but this did not smell like Thorn at all. This was more like—

"It's Berry!" gasped Sky, taking two rapid steps forward.

Shocked, Fearless swept his paw across the torn body, dislodging more flowers and revealing its identity. Her face was oddly peaceful, and emotions warred within his heart. *Berry too? This is unbearable. But where is Thorn's body?*

He tore his eyes from Berry. Fearless had grown up with her; it was her father, Stinger, who had snatched him from the eagle's nest when he was a cub. Berry had been his friend. They had drifted apart recently, torn by the conflicts that ravaged all of Bravelands, but they had never truly lost that affection that bound them together. Berry had been one of the cleverest baboons he knew; she'd had all her father's intelligence with none of his malice.

He realized in that moment that the peaceful future he'd imagined—when he, Berry, and Thorn might sit in a glade together and laugh about old times—would never be.

He became aware of two shadows, slinking cautiously out of the undergrowth. He glanced toward them, alert for hostility from Dawntrees Troop. But there were only two baboons, and one of them cleared his throat as he padded into a patch of sunlight.

"Hello, Big Talk," he said.

"Nut," exclaimed Fearless. "It's you!"

"And this is Spider," said Nut, with a glance at the skinny baboon behind him, its tail crooked, its gaze wide and a little vague.

Neither of them looked particularly distraught, which made no sense at all. Unless of course . . . *they don't know!*

How could he break the news to them? Fearless shot a desperate glance to Sky, hoping she might be the one to tell Thorn's friends the awful truth. From the sorrow in her gaze, he guessed she was willing him to do the same. *Very well*, he thought. *It's my duty, as friend to Dawntrees.*

"Nut," he said softly. "I have something I must tell you." He struggled then to continue. How could he share the wretched tale without breaking their poor hearts? "It's Thorn," he mumbled. "He's . . . he's dead."

The reaction wasn't as he suspected at all. Nut hesitated, exchanging a glance of trepidation with his odd companion. For a moment they muttered to each other, so softly that Fearless could hear only an occasional word: *secret* and *promised* and then, finally, *trust.*

Nut cleared his throat again and padded closer to the lion and the two elephants. He glanced from side to side and peered cautiously into the tree shadows. Quietly he said, "Thorn lives."

Sky shifted awkwardly behind Fearless. They couldn't accept the truth; it was hardly a surprise. "I'm sorry to be the one to tell you," said Fearless. "But I heard it from Titan's own mouth. It isn't a lie he would tell."

Nut looked unmoved. "It isn't a lie as such," he said, "but Titan is mistaken. We were with Thorn just a short while ago. He's in hiding."

"But how?" exclaimed Sky. "The wolves said they ate his heart!"

"They attacked what they *thought* was the Great Parent." Nut's expression grew grim and dark. "Berry tricked them into thinking it was her. She—she did it behind Thorn's back, to save his life." His voice broke, and he fell silent.

Spider glanced at Nut, anxious. Then he gazed up at Sky. "Poor Thorn-friend," he murmured. "He didn't know. Berry Crownleaf did a brave thing."

"She did." Sky's voice was somber. "She lost her own life, but she saved the Great Father's."

"That at least is good news," murmured Rock, curling his trunk around Sky's.

Things were moving so fast that Fearless felt dizzy. "I'm glad Thorn is alive," he rasped, "but his heart must be in pieces. I've known Berry all my life. She was kind to me from the moment I was brought into Brightforest Troop. She was the best of baboons. And she . . . she was so dear to Thorn, for so long."

"I can't bear to think how he'll be feeling," said Sky quietly.

"Nut," said Fearless. "What can we do to help him? I feel we have to do *something*."

"Don't worry," said Nut grimly. "Thorn will need all the help he can get, and he'll need it soon. We can all show our support for him then."

"He'll call on us before long." Spider nodded. "Spider feels it."

"Where is Dawntrees Troop now?" asked Sky suddenly. She reached her trunk upward and gently lifted down the baby baboon. It was wide-awake, and it gazed around the animals with huge frightened eyes. "Don't worry, little one," Sky murmured to it. "We're going to help you." She held up the baby, cradled in her trunk, to show the others. "She was in the fire. We need to find her a mother, and I thought there might be someone in Dawntrees who's willing to help. She has to nurse soon, or she'll die."

"That infant looks familiar . . ." murmured Nut, peering with fascination at the tiny baboon.

"It's Tendril's baby, Seedling," agreed Spider. "Spider recognizes that fur-splash on its head." He pointed to the patch of black fur like a splayed leaf.

"I think you're right." Nut frowned. "I thought she would have died after Creeper and Viper murdered her mother. Spider and I will help find her a new one."

Fearless watched as the two baboons cooed over the tiny creature in Sky's trunk. Life had always been fragile in Bravelands, but looking at the helpless little baboon, Fearless knew it had become an incredibly precarious thing now. It could be snatched away at any moment, by enemies that had never been expected or foreseen—like those Codebreaking golden wolves.

What started all this in Bravelands? he wondered. Stinger had turned all their lives upside down, it was true, but even that wicked baboon had never tried to steal the spirits of the dead. He had never allied with a pack as demented and savage as the wolves. No, it was Titan who had brought Bravelands so low, Titan who strode across the savannah consuming spirits, making himself ever stronger and ever more insane, never caring about what he did or the effect it would have on the whole land. How could Thorn and his friends ever hope to defeat such a creature? Baboons stood no chance against Titan.

But lions might, he realized. *We're the only ones with any chance of stopping him.*

"Sky," he said, turning to her, "can you get a message to me when Thorn contacts the other animals? I need to go back to my pride, and the lions don't always hear of Great Gatherings."

"Of course." She touched his neck with the tip of her trunk. "Though I think that when Thorn makes his move, you will be one of the first he seeks out, Fearless. We will leave this place soon, too." She glanced at the sky, and at the dark silhouettes hunched in the branches above them. "The vultures will want to be about their proper business."

"Yes," agreed Fearless sadly. "Take care, Sky and Rock. We *all* need to be careful these days."

"May the Great Spirit go with you, my friend," she said.

Fearless set out through the forest toward his waiting pride;

he found himself, almost without thinking, walking even more carefully than usual, placing his paws as silently as he could, tensing at the smallest sound of tiny creeping animals. All of Bravelands seemed to tremble, like a shriveled leaf that hung precariously to a creaking branch.

When he reached his pride, most of them lay sprawled in the grass just beyond the forest's edge, but all were alert and watchful. Heads turned to watch him approach, and ears pricked toward him.

"The Great Father lives after all, Great Spirit be praised," he said.

Some of the lions rolled their eyes and muttered at that comment, but Fearless took no notice. "But I've made a decision. The threat Titan poses to Bravelands is still huge, and Thorn can't deal with him alone."

"Only lions can deal with lions," drawled Resolute.

"My thoughts exactly," said Fearless, narrowing his eyes.

"But some of us have only just escaped Titan," Resolute went on. "We don't plan to go back for more punishment."

"Titan had so much power because the other prides were smaller and weaker," insisted Fearless. "If lions join together to defeat him, he won't be able to stand against us. Mighty-pride, for instance. I think they will stand with us. Mighty doesn't like bullies any more than I do, and he knows what a danger Titan poses. That's what we need—for prides to band together, and defeat Titan as one!"

"Is it, though?" growled Resolute. "Is that *really* what we need?"

"Or," added a young former lioness of Titanpride, "do we need to find ourselves a territory that's far from Titan, and leave this baboon Father of yours to deal with him?"

"Sounds far more sensible to me," grunted the lion at her side. "Isn't that what the grass-eaters and the little cats keep a Great Parent for? To solve all their problems?"

"You don't understand at all," snapped Fearless. "No, that's not what a Great Father is, whether you believe in the Great Spirit or not. Thorn is a guide and a protector, but he can't do it all alone. No one could."

Resolute yawned. "Still not our problem. Titan's one lone male, and he'll shake off those silly wolves soon enough. He's no threat to us if we stay within our territory, and frankly, Fearless, that's what matters. Lions have no responsibility to protect—oh, warthogs and ground squirrels."

"No," snarled Ruthless, padding to Fearless's side. "You're wrong, Resolute. You might have been in his pride, but you clearly don't know my father at all. There's nowhere you can go, in or beyond Bravelands, where you'd be safe from Titan. He's mad, don't you realize that yet? He'll go on spreading his madness till there're no lands or territories left for him to conquer."

"That's as may be," said an older lion nervously, scratching at a scar on his forepaw, "but however much we hate Titan, we're not strong enough to defeat him. You can't be certain that other lions will join you, Fearless. It sounds like guaranteed destruction to me."

"And leaving Titan alone doesn't come to the same thing?"

exploded Fearless. "Look at it this way: Titan's obsession is killing. Not eating, just murdering. He slays for hearts and spirits, not for meat! And that means he'll kill and kill regardless—he *and* that wolf pack of his. They'll never be satisfied, and there will be no prey left when they're finished. Maybe they'll starve in the end, but *you will starve first.* We all will."

The lions exchanged glances. Resolute looked surly, but he nodded. "Now, there's a point to *that* argument."

"I agree," muttered Glory.

"Fearless is right." Ruthless looked solemnly around the pride. "Deep down you know it, whether you care about the other animals or not. Sure, Resolute, we might not need to worry about 'warthogs and ground squirrels.' But we'll care a lot when there are none left to eat."

"Wise words, Titan's cub," said Resolute reluctantly. "I think we can all see the sense. All right, Fearless, we're with you." He glanced around at his comrades, who growled agreement.

"You should be," Fearless reminded them sharply. "You're Fearlesspride now, remember?" He turned without another word, to stride off toward the east and Mightypride territory. For long moments his breath felt jerky and his heart juddered, but he would not look back. He couldn't; he must look confident at all costs.

But his head swam with relief when he heard the pride fall into line behind him, their obedient paws crunching on the dry grass.

He had to be sure of himself, he knew. His new pride was

hungry, and many of the lionesses had cubs in tow. They wanted meat, and the hunt, and a normal lion life. At some point, he would have to provide it for them, or Fearlesspride would fracture and collapse—perhaps at the cost of his own life.

Ruthless caught up with him, jogging at his side. "I'm sorry, Fearless," he said quietly.

"What for?" Fearless flicked his ears quizzically. "You supported me very well back there."

"No. For ruining your fight with Titan," said Ruthless. "If I hadn't been stupid enough to get cornered by the wolves—"

"It wasn't your fault," Fearless assured him, though the memory of his frustration turned his voice to a deep growl. "Titan always has lieutenants to back him up, and to save his worthless hide when he's in trouble. He'd have had that plan set up before he even ran into me. That's why we have to be clever when we fight him."

"I understand—" Ruthless halted abruptly, his nostrils flaring. "Fearless, I smell antelope!"

Fearless followed the turn of his head, excitement rising. A hunt would distract his pride from their troubles, fill their bellies, and make them far more likely to follow him. And Ruthless was right; a herd was moving slowly to their left. A few sentries scanned the grassland, broad and elegant horns raised high, but there was no indication that they had noticed the lions.

"Yes," he murmured. "Impalas—I see them!"

"They're fast," said Ruthless, "but there are enough of us to take one."

Turning, Fearless slunk back to Glory. "Get the others into position," he growled. "See the impalas? We're going to hunt."

Her eyes lit up with hungry excitement, and she twisted and loped back, shoulders and haunches low, to spread the word through the pride. They had done little hunting as a team, but all the lions swiftly and without apparent trouble separated themselves into groups for right and left flank, and for harrying from behind. Fearless felt his heart swell with pleasure.

His hopes rose as the lions fanned out and slunk swiftly into position, hemming in the herd from the rear and sides. Some seemed to sense the danger, but from the restless way their hooves skittered, Fearless realized they still hadn't actually seen the approaching hunters. Then a few impalas began to trot, followed by others; Fearless saw Glory and Ruthless picking up speed to the left, eyeing the grass-eaters keenly to judge their speed and direction.

As the herd sprang into flight, Fearless picked up speed. Oddly, one impala ran at a different angle from the rest, racing perilously close to his hunting trajectory. *Well*, he thought, *there's no accounting for the behavior of grass-eaters. More fool than impala.*

As Fearless homed in on it he saw another blur of gold aiming for the same prey at a sharper angle. The impala spotted the other lion, and panic sparked in its eyes, but in its dash to elude the hunter it was running right across Fearless's sight line.

Accelerating, Fearless bunched his haunches and leaped, just as it finally caught sight of him. It tried to dodge at the last moment, but his claws dug deep into its rump, dragging it down. It stumbled, kicking in desperation, and from the corner of his eye he saw the other lion bolting to join him.

It's doomed. It can't escape. We will eat!

The lion barreled into the antelope from its other flank, but as Fearless triumphantly dug his claws deeper and lunged for its throat with his jaws, the newcomer gave a snarl and swiped at his head with exposed claws.

For a fraction of an instant, Fearless didn't understand. The lion must be one of his; he even smelled familiar! Fearless swung his head and bared his fangs to snarl a warning.

Then he realized. *Keen!* His once closest friend and he had parted on cold terms when Keen, frustrated by Fearless's obsession with Titan, had left to join Mightypride. At the sight of him, Fearless felt his heart soar; he couldn't help it. His snarl faded into a growl of surprise.

Keen, though, showed no sign of lingering affection. "Get away from my kill!" he roared.

"*Your* kill?" Narrowing his eyes, Fearless got ahold of himself. He peeled back his muzzle, distracted by the need to hang on to the impala. It still kicked and struggled, and he could feel the strain in his claws as it tried to rip itself free.

"Why do you think it ran straight toward you?" demanded Keen. "I've been stalking it! Get off my prey!"

The impala collapsed at last, worn out, and Keen clamped his jaws around its neck, even as he went on glaring at Fearless. The rest of Fearless's pride was running closer, and Fearless realized he had only a moment to make his decision.

Reluctantly, with a wrench of disappointment, he stepped away. "Leave it," he growled to Ruthless and Resolute, and they stared at him in disbelief. "The kill belongs to Keen."

"Where's the rest of his pride, then?" snarled Resolute.

Keen dropped the impala's broken neck. "I was out alone. I came across the herd and decided to have a go. I cut this one off before you all came on the scene. It's mine."

And I doubt you'd have caught it if we hadn't blocked its escape. Fearless took a breath to say it, but the glare of defiance in Keen's brown eyes made him hesitate.

"And you're in Mightypride territory!" snapped Keen. "You shouldn't even be here."

Fearless curled his muzzle. He didn't want to fight with Keen, not the very first time he'd seen him after their ill-tempered parting. His heart felt too full at the sight of his old friend, however cold the hostility in Keen's eyes.

"It's Keen's," he growled in a low voice.

"Ridiculous," snapped Glory, who had trotted up, salivating.

"Nevertheless, I'm your leader," snarled Fearless. "Let him take it back to Mightypride."

For a moment, he wasn't sure if the other lions were going to heed his instruction. Their fur bristled and their eyes were fixed on the fresh meat before them. Perhaps in a more established pride they'd have listened straightaway, but his grip on power was tenuous at best.

"Come," he said, trying to sound more authoritative. "We'll find another."

"I'll believe that when my fangs are in its rump," muttered Glory. Turning, she stalked back to the rest of the pride, who were muttering among themselves and glaring at both Fearless and Keen.

With a slight, cold nod, Keen sank his teeth into the impala's neck and braced himself to drag it away. Then his shoulders stiffened, and his eyes found Fearless's again.

"Thank you," he grunted reluctantly.

"Keen." Fearless took a breath. "Will you take me to Mighty?"

The young lion narrowed his eyes, releasing his hold on the impala. "He won't be pleased to see you."

"I know it's unusual, but we have important things to discuss with him. We didn't intend to hunt on his territory. We had not crossed the boundary when we began." Fearless took a hesitant pace toward his old friend. "Let me approach him, Keen. Please?"

"Fine," growled Keen after a moment. "But don't say I didn't warn you."

"Fearless, is this wise?" put in Ruthless, glancing anxiously from him to Keen.

"Mighty is proud, but he's fair and he's smart," Fearless assured him. He raised his voice to address his pride. "The rest of you, stay here on the edge of Mighty's territory."

His pride watched him go with a mixture of anger, suspicion, and resentment. For a moment Fearless thought how it must look to them: he was entering possibly hostile territory to meet with another pride leader, and he was helping a member of that pride drag away an impala that should have been theirs.

He shook off the anxiety. He couldn't afford to dwell on their response to this odd situation. Any problems with his own pride, he could solve later. For now it was more important to consult with Mighty about the threats that faced Bravelands. Fearless sank his jaws more firmly around the impala's shoulder and put extra effort into helping Keen carry it.

The impala was heavy, and it was long, hard work; Fearless wondered how far away Mightypride could be. How big *was* this territory? Neither he nor Keen could spare the breath to exchange any words, even if their jaws hadn't been full of impala. The farther they dragged it from Fearlesspride, the more vulnerable Fearless felt. But he couldn't let himself be distracted from his mission. *Mighty will understand why I'm here.*

His hide prickled as he became aware of watching eyes; Mightypride scouts rose from the concealing grass to stare at him as he dragged the impala at Keen's side.

"Leave it here," growled Keen at last, dropping the prey.

Nodding, Fearless released the impala, and as he padded on with Keen, he glanced back to see the scouts home in on the carcass. They would take it the rest of the way, he realized, and Mightypride would feast today . . . while Fearlesspride went hungry.

Uncertainty rippled through his gut, but he swallowed hard and paced after Keen. Ahead lay a cluster of shady acacias, and he could make out the shapes of recumbent lionesses. They rose as he and Keen approached, and stalked aggressively forward, their teeth bared. At least eight sleek lionesses fanned out to face him, snarling in threat. If they took exception to the presence of a rogue male and chose to attack, he'd have little chance to escape alive.

Then, beyond them, Fearless saw the pride leader rise, stretch, and turn. Mighty looked bigger than ever, his mane thick and magnificent. His golden eyes met Fearless's, and they were not welcoming.

"What is the meaning of this?" growled Mighty.

There was no trace of the kindness and geniality that Fearless remembered. Mighty looked hostile, strong, and completely in control. He took three deliberate paces toward Fearless, his mane bristling, his fangs gleaming.

"Answer me, Fearless. Why have you entered my territory? You are not welcome here."

Fearless halted. He couldn't help but swallow hard, as a lurch of fear clenched his chest.

He had to think hard about his answer, and he had to do it fast. Because he knew, with certainty, that the wrong words would be the death of him.

CHAPTER FIVE

Sky was very conscious of the tiny baboon on her back; as she made her way through the forest ahead of Rock, she had to be careful not to let branches snap back and hurt the little creature. She chose her path carefully, searching for the clearest route through the tangle of vines and undergrowth, ducking the lowest boughs as well as she could. The baby stirred occasionally, but weakly, and it had stopped crying out with hunger and fear. Not, Sky thought, because the poor thing didn't still feel them, but because she no longer had the strength to protest.

In fact, it wasn't a branch that dislodged the baby; she simply lost her grip suddenly and slipped from Sky's back. Though she was lighter than a starling feather, Sky was instantly aware she was gone, and gave a cry of alarm.

Sky turned as fast as she could, but Rock had caught the little baboon as she fell. She saw with relief that he cradled her fragile body in his trunk. The baby's eyelids flickered and trembled, but they didn't open.

"We haven't got long, Sky," he rumbled. "We have to find her a mother, soon."

Very tentatively, Sky extended her trunk and blew gently onto the baby's muzzle. "Little one," she crooned, "try to stay awake."

With what seemed an enormous effort, the baby opened her heavy eyelids, blinking up at Sky. Her eyes were huge in her emaciated face, but she couldn't emit so much as a whimper.

Rock set her carefully back on Sky's shoulders, leaving his trunk-tip curled around the baby to steady her. "Let's try to move a little faster, Sky. I'll stop her falling."

As she turned, Sky heard a rustling and creaking in the branches above her. Glancing up, she saw furred shadows leaping between the trees, following their path through the forest.

"Baboons," she whispered to Rock. "They're watching us."

"Well, we did come looking for them," he said. "Let's just hope they're friendly."

They must be very close to the heart of Dawntrees territory now, Sky thought with trepidation. Taking a breath, she parted a tangle of vines and stepped forward into a broad, sun-dappled glade.

She halted, with a tremor of uncertainty. Baboons were everywhere. On low branches, on mounds of earth and rotten logs, gathered in clusters gossiping or gnawing on fruits, they all fell silent and turned toward the two elephants. In the center of the clearing stood a huge, flat-topped boulder, and on it lounged a one-eyed, grizzled baboon with a surly expression.

"Greetings. Are you . . ." Sky cleared her throat. "Are you the Dawntrees Troop?"

Slowly, almost lazily, the baboon rose to his paws, eyeing her. "I am Creeper Highleaf."

"I . . . I see." Sky's hide was hot with the awkwardness of the moment. "Greetings to you, Creeper Highleaf. I am Sky Strider, and my mate Rock and I have come to ask for your help, but also to deliver upsetting news."

Creeper stared at her for a long moment, his single eye traveling from her feet to her shoulders. He squinted and frowned.

"That's a young baboon," he grunted. "What are you doing with it?"

"I will come to that," said Sky. She lowered her eyelashes. "But know first that Berry Crownleaf is dead. She was killed by Titan the lion and his pack of wolves."

There was an eruption of distressed hoots from the baboons around the clearing, and cries of dismay and disbelief.

"Berry Crownleaf?"

"No!"

"Oh, may the Great Spirit take her to the stars."

"Mama, is it true?" whimpered an older youngling. "Berry's dead?"

In the hubbub, Sky watched Creeper, but he simply gazed back at her, unperturbed. He turned his head toward his friends. "Hey, Viper. Hear that? Berry Crownleaf's dead."

"Hmph." The muscular female called Viper strutted to his side. "She wasn't Berry *Crownleaf*, though, was she? Not anymore."

"What?" said Sky, startled.

"That's right." Creeper nodded and picked his teeth. "She was Berry Deeproot when she left."

"Demoted by the Crown Guard, as is our right." Viper shrugged.

"We get rid of useless leaders," put in a male beside her. "Works very well. Keeps a leader on their toes."

"Mm-hmm." Viper nodded. "And if she's dead now, it proves we Crown Guard were right. She was weak all along."

"No!" Sky couldn't contain her horror anymore. "Berry was no weak leader—how can you think that?" Around her baboons of the troop fell silent, some of them listening sympathetically, others glaring with resentment—especially the Crown Guard around Creeper. "The Great Father loved Berry!"

"Oh, *him*," sneered Viper. "He's still alive, is he? Saved his own skin?"

Sky clenched her jaws, trying not to swipe her trunk at the snide baboon. "He's alive, yes— thank the Spirit. Thorn knows Titan is everyone's enemy. And even now, he's working on a plan to bring that evil lion down."

The Crown Guard couldn't contain themselves at that; they hooted and slapped the ground with laughter. "Good luck with that!" shrieked another sturdy male.

"Thorn couldn't even control his own baboon troop," howled Viper.

Creeper peeled back his lips in a hostile grin. "He's got no chance. Maybe Titan will eat him quickly."

Sky stared at them all, shocked. "He wasn't your leader, but don't you have any respect for him as the Great Father?"

"Great Father?" mocked another Crown Guard baboon, leaping up onto a branch. "Great Coward, more like!"

"Great Slugwit," giggled another, skinnier baboon.

"Good one, Fang." Creeper laughed.

Sky swallowed back the sickened feeling. What had happened to the baboons and their traditions?

"Anyway," continued Creeper. "You still haven't explained about the baboon clinging to your boyfriend. Tell him to release it at once!"

Rock glared at him, but Sky kept her voice as humble as she could. "He can't, Creeper. It'll fall. The poor thing is so weak."

"Why? What have you done to it?" Creeper rose up on his hind paws, glaring.

"Nothing," snapped Rock.

"We, uh . . ." Sky thought fast. "We found it in the great destruction to the west, where fire-flowers ate the forest. It has no mother; she must have died in the flames and smoke."

Creeper tilted his head and gazed at the baby, rather dispassionately. The other baboons were loping closer, muttering among themselves and pointing at the infant. Some gave soft cries of sympathy; others grunted and chittered their fangs.

"Ordinarily," said Creeper at last, "I'd tell you to leave it for the rot-eaters. That'd be the natural thing." He shrugged. "But Dawntrees needs more members, that's the truth." He glanced at a couple of other strong-looking baboons, who nodded. "We've lost many young ourselves recently. We have bereaved mothers who'd be happy to take the youngling."

"That would be generous and noble," Sky flattered him.

"Hmph. It'd be advantageous for the troop, or I wouldn't consider it." Creeper raised his voice and barked. "Scratcher!"

A female baboon hurried forward from the crowd, her mournful brown eyes lighting up with hope. "Yes, Creeper?"

"Didn't you lose an infant? Do you want this one?"

Scratcher stared up at the baby and nodded eagerly. She opened her arms as Rock lifted the tiny thing down, and she took it from him with great care. For a moment, mother and baby gazed at each other, wide-eyed and nervous. Then Scratcher stroked the baby's skull and cuddled its scrawny body close to her.

"Thank you," she whispered to Rock.

The baby's tiny claws clutched tightly onto Scratcher's fur, clinging for dear life, and Sky felt a wave of relief as she began to nurse hungrily.

"She is well enough to feed," murmured Scratcher, looking ecstatic. "She will survive. Blessed be the Great Spirit."

"I'm so glad," murmured Sky.

"I shall call her . . ." Scratcher hesitated and glanced down at the little baboon. "Greenshoot. Because she brought me new life and hope."

"A fine name," rumbled Rock.

Scratcher has that right, thought Sky, sadly. *But poor Tendril: snatched by the fire from her baby, and now even the name she gave her will be lost.*

But this was what Sky and Rock had searched for: a mother who would care. Little Greenshoot would live now and be loved. Sky smiled. "Yes, Scratcher, that name was well chosen—"

"Is that all?" interrupted Creeper, scratching with irritation at the scar of his empty eye socket. "Because it's time you were leaving." There were hoots of agreement from the powerful baboons behind him, and something struck Sky's shoulder; as it shattered and splashed pulp, she realized it was a rotten mango. It didn't hurt, but deep inside she felt the sting of anger. Rock gave a bellow of fury and fanned out his ears.

"I'll tear your nests down," he blared.

"No." Sky stepped a little in front of him. She stared around at Dawntrees Troop, and then up at the Crown Guard who had taken to the trees. Some of them held more overripe mangoes, and they were grinning.

"They're ignorant brutes," Rock growled.

"Yes, and they're not worth a fight," said Sky, clearly and calmly. She looked at Creeper, who had bounded back onto the Crown Stone. "We have more important battles to fight, Rock. Let's go."

Mangoes thudded and splattered on the ground behind them as she and Rock marched out of the clearing, and Sky heard baboon jeers fading behind them as she made her way out of the forest, toward the secret ravine that Nut and Mud had told them about. None of Dawntrees Troop followed them; the Crown Guard didn't have quite enough nerve for *that*, she thought contemptuously.

There was a quiet fury inside her: *How dare they talk about the Great Parent like that? How dare they disrespect Berry's memory?* She and Rock had been right to walk away; Creeper and the Crown Guard were not worth his justified wrath.

But alongside the anger, there was a rising anxiety, a cold and creeping fear for the future.

Those baboons cared nothing for the Great Spirit, or the traditions of Bravelands, or the Great Parent's authority.

How long might it be before such contempt spread to infect all of Bravelands?

CHAPTER SIX

Mighty stalked forward. Sunlight made his pelt and his mane glow with what seemed like a Spirit-given magnificence. And Fearless's argument was not with him; it was definitely no time to fight. Fearless dipped his head, lowered his tail, and swung his body aside, crouching submissively.

His breath was in his throat. Mighty could still attack, of course, and he wouldn't even be ready to dodge. Though fear clutched at his gut, he forced himself not to meet Mighty's glare.

Mighty halted. All Fearless could see, a little in front of his muzzle, were Mighty's colossal paws. His whiskers twitched with nerves. Those long and powerful claws had sprung out of their sheaths.

"I do not come to challenge you," Fearless said, as meekly as he could. "I come to you in peace, Mighty, because I need to talk to you. About something that threatens all of us—every Bravelands pride."

Mighty's claws raked deeper into the red earth, but he didn't lunge. Fearless risked glancing up, to meet his eyes at last.

He licked his dry jaws. "Titan is alive, Mighty, and more dangerous than ever. He's *stronger* than ever, and he's made an alliance with the golden wolves. It's time for true lions to come together." Fearless gulped. "I came here to warn you, Mighty, nothing more. I want us to agree to a truce—an alliance. We can protect one another."

"Titan's more dangerous?" Mighty's deep rumble was skeptical, and a little threatening. "That's not what I've heard. My scouts tell me that he's lost his entire pride." He paused. "To *you.*"

Fearless blinked. He was reluctant to admit that he had not taken his brand-new pride in a traditional fight, that the lions had actually left Titan's control for a quieter life.

But right now, appeasing Mighty was more important than Fearless's dignity. "That's not . . . not quite what happened," he said through gritted teeth.

"But you have Titan's pride." Mighty tilted his head. "They're yours."

"Yes, but—"

"There are those who would say," Mighty interrupted smoothly, "that I should kill you on the spot, Fearless. Not just for your insolence in coming onto my territory, but to protect my pride in the future."

Fearless fell silent under Mighty's piercing glare; it seemed like the best strategy right now. He had not expected this, and he had not planned his reaction. Mighty had once been easy-going and good-natured; pride leadership must have taught him to be far more aggressive and suspicious.

"Mighty . . . I respect you as leader of your pride. I respect your authority, and I have no wish to challenge it, now or in the future." Fearless felt his heart beating rapidly. "In normal times I would never have come here, I promise you. But these are not normal times, not for any animal in Bravelands. Titan does still have a pride—but a pride of wolves! How is that right?"

"Wolves?" Mighty gave a grunting, menacing laugh. "I don't fear wolves!"

"You should," said Fearless quietly.

It was the wrong thing to say, and Fearless knew it immediately. Mighty drew himself up, his muscles rippling beneath his pelt. Fearless had never really taken in before how *massive* he was.

"Who are you," growled Mighty, "that you stride into my territory and tell me what I should fear? Who are you, Fearless, to think you can make me afraid of *anything* you choose?" He placed one huge paw deliberately forward. "I have put up with you this long, cub, for your sister Valor's sake. But I will *not* be ordered around by an immature male who's only just sprouted a mane!"

Fearless found himself trembling, but he made a huge effort to hold his ground, gazing up at Mighty. *I'm not that much smaller than he is. And my mane is almost full!* Slowly, he calmed his breathing. "I apologize, Mighty. I shouldn't have said what I did. But I know Titan, and I've seen with my own eyes what he's capable of. He kills animals only so that he can take their spirits into himself. He eats their hearts, and with every one he grows more powerful. And he has eaten *many* hearts."

"And I am Mighty." With a thunderous roar, the huge lion struck the ground with a paw, sending up a cloud of dust. "If Titan dares to enter my territory, I won't show him the same forbearance I've shown you. I will kill him."

What could he say? Fearless thought. Mighty refused to be told, it was as simple as that. There was silence on the plain as all of Mightypride watched him, and the sun beating down on his back felt heavy and oppressive. Even Keen did not rush to his support, as he would have in the past.

But why would he, now? It's not how it was, and it never will be again.

Again Fearless wondered, with a strange and sad detachment, how many friends he would lose to his quest to bring down Titan. It didn't matter. Or it did, but it couldn't be helped.

"How is Valor?" he asked quietly at last. "It's been so long since I've seen her." He turned his head to peer at the lions in the long grass, then at the ones who sprawled in the acacia shade, but there was no sign of his sister. Would this new, hostile Mighty even tell him if something had happened to her?

"Your sister is well," growled Mighty. "I shall give her your regards, Fearless. And now you must leave."

"Wait, Mighty." Keen padded forward to stand at Fearless's side. "Fearless helped me bring down that impala, and he gave it up to me against the wishes of his own pride. Perhaps we should listen to him."

Fearless was so surprised, he could only turn his head and blink at his former friend. So Keen *was* standing up for him. His heart clenched.

Keen gave him a glance that was unreadable. "I can vouch for Fearless, Mighty. He hasn't come here out of aggression. He loves his sister, he understands the bonds of blood, and he's no threat to your cubs."

Fearless sucked in a breath of shock and delight. "Cubs?"

Mighty glowered at Keen, then at Fearless. "Yes. Valor has two cubs."

"I'm . . . Mighty, I'm happy for you. And I'm sorry—of course you don't want males of other prides around." *No wonder he's been so aggressive.* Fearless dipped his head humbly. "But I swear to you, I would never hurt Valor's offspring. Please, may I see her?"

Mighty was silent for what seemed a very long time. Only the very tip of his tail twitched, as if in an agony of indecision. Then he turned without a word and stalked off to a flowering acacia with a broad spreading crown. It wasn't a refusal, and that was enough.

Fearless followed, his heart in his mouth. Several lionesses sprawled in the shade of the branches, and none of them looked well fed; some were downright skinny. But he saw Valor immediately, and she looked relatively healthy. Her head came up as he approached, and she rose swiftly to her paws.

"Fearless? Is it really you?"

"Valor!" He bounded toward her, ignoring Mighty's warning growl, and they fell to licking each other on the face and neck. "Oh, sister, it's good to see you again!"

"It's been too long," she agreed, swiping her tongue across his cheek.

Fearless felt suddenly shy. "You look more like our mother than ever, Valor." It was true: her always-fierce face had matured, taking on the nobility and kindness that had characterized Swift.

"And you are growing up fast, little brother." Valor gave a low, fond laugh. "You're far stronger than when I last saw you. And I'd swear there's a mane coming in."

"It's taking its time." Fearless panted and rolled his eyes. "But Valor, I hear you have cubs?"

She lay down again, very gently, and nudged a little head that appeared from the dry grass. The cub gazed at Fearless, unafraid, with huge dark eyes. In a moment or two, another head popped up, edging shyly closer to its sibling.

Fearless felt a rush of instinctive affection and delight. "They're fine Valorcubs," he told Valor softly, then turned to Mighty. "You must be proud."

"Oh, we are," said Mighty, in a guarded tone.

Valor glanced up at Mighty, her golden eyes warm with love. "It's all right, Mighty. Fearless wouldn't do us harm."

"Very well." The great lion stooped to lick her head and ears. "I should get back to the rest of the pride. Keen has brought in an impala, and I don't want the young males to eat the whole thing."

The cubs began to suckle at Valor's belly; Fearless watched, mesmerized. "The Great Spirit is good," he murmured. "New life in Mightypride!"

"The Great Spirit," said Valor dryly, "had nothing to do with it." She pulled a face at Fearless. "Do you still believe in all that, brother? Really?"

"You know what?" Fearless laughed, finding himself unconcerned by her mockery. "I really do."

"Please yourself," she purred, and let him lick her ear. "That's what comes from being raised by baboons, I guess."

"It wasn't only that," said Fearless. "Brightforest Troop only introduced me to the idea. The rest, I have seen for myself. We lions rarely have to wonder why or how Bravelands prospers. What we want, we take." He hesitated. "But the Great Spirit has more power than any creature, and we need its help. Especially now."

Valor looked more solemn. She gazed at him. "You're still worried?"

"I am," he told her grimly. "Titan lives, and he'll be a threat to Bravelands for as long as he's breathing."

"It's not just your desire for revenge that's telling you this, little brother?"

He shook his head. "No. I have my own reasons for wanting him dead, Valor; of course I do. And I swore to put an end to him. But it's more than that. Titan threatens *everything*." He took a breath and bent his head to lick the braver cub. It mewled imperiously at him. "He's even a danger to little ones like these."

Valor studied him again, then glanced down at her cubs. "Not while I'm alive," she said quietly. Then she glanced back up at him, her eyes lighting up with gentle amusement once more. "Ah, brother. I always knew you'd tread a strange path through life, but I could never have predicted just *how* strange."

"Fearless." Mighty's deep voice rang out behind them once more. "You've had time enough. You must leave now."

Reluctantly, Fearless nodded. It had been such a brief time with his sister, and he couldn't help a surge of resentful disappointment, but he had no choice. He turned to face the pride leader.

"Thank you, Mighty," he said, lowering his head and tail again. "I'm happy you let me see Valor and her—your cubs."

"Don't come here unannounced again," Mighty warned him. With a jerk of his head he beckoned the young lion behind him. "Keen will escort you from our territory."

Fearless could see there was no point arguing. He had failed in his mission, and there would be no alliance. Still, Fearless couldn't help a small twinge of happiness as he followed Keen away from the acacia grove.

It was good to see Valor and her cubs, he thought.

"Mightypride seems happy," Fearless ventured, after what seemed a long interval of silence. Keen padded just ahead of him, his tail twitching with what looked like nerves. The savannah shimmered before the two young lions as they crested a low ridge and began to jog down to the flat plain. A silver river looped across it, still and gleaming.

"We are," said Keen. He gave a sigh and finally slowed his

pace so that he was walking alongside Fearless. "Mighty is a fine leader, Fearless. He's tough, but he's fair. And there are several new cubs. The pride has a good future, I think."

"You think?" Fearless glanced at him. He could tell Keen was troubled; he was concealing something.

Keen made a grunting noise in his throat. "I won't be disloyal to Mighty," he growled.

Fearless opened his jaws, then closed them again. They walked on for a little way farther without speaking.

At last Keen turned his head once again. "I'm not lying, Fearless; Mighty is a good leader. But I can't deny we've had our share of bad luck lately. Valor's our best hunter, but she's been out of action. And another good lioness was killed."

"Killed?" Fearless flicked his ears.

"Just one of those things: an unlucky kick from an ostrich. The wound was deep, and it went bad. She died within days." Keen's expression was dark. "But things are still good." He was silent again for long moments. "I mean, they could be worse. Mighty won't hear of any disheartening talk."

Fearless said nothing, afraid of offending Keen again, but he could tell how disturbed his old friend was. There was a lot Keen wasn't saying, he decided. Valor *was* a fine hunter, and the pride must be missing her full abilities. To lose another lioness at the same time was the worst of luck.

"I wish I could help," he said at last, remembering the skinniness of the nursing lionesses.

"Well," said Keen, halting, "you can't. That river is the boundary of Mightypride's land." Awkwardly he added, "It was good to see you, Fearless. Actually, very good."

Fearless turned to gaze at him. "Listen, Keen. Maybe there's nothing I can do to help, but will you let me try? I have fine hunters in my pride."

"They're going to want to hunt for themselves," Keen pointed out. "For Fearlesspride. What would there be in it for them and for you?"

"I'm their leader," insisted Fearless. "And I *do* want something from Mighty: his help. His support. If I could marshal a hunt to get prey for Mightypride, he might believe that I really do want an alliance." He took a breath. "What do you think, Keen?"

"What do I think of another crazy plan from Fearless the baboon-lion?" There was reluctant amusement in Keen's eyes, and something more—a spark of optimism.

"Go on, Keen. It's worth a try, isn't it?" Fearless tilted his head encouragingly.

"Very well." Keen gave a grunting bark of laughter. "You know what, Fearless? I think this particular crazy idea might be one of your better ones. However grumpy he acts these days, Mighty's the same good-hearted lion he always was. It's worth a shot."

"So you'll help me?" asked Fearless eagerly.

"When did I ever refuse?" Keen replied.

CHAPTER SEVEN

As he climbed, Thorn placed a paw on a smooth white rock that jutted from the ground near the lip of the ravine. He had always touched this stone as he padded down into the gully, without thinking; it had been a convenient resting place for a forepaw. Now the plain rock seemed to vibrate with memories and meaning. There was the straggly fever tree, clinging to fissures in the rock that had shaded them as they embraced. There was the flat boulder where she used to wait for him, her face upturned and radiant with joy. There was the patch of scree and loose boulders where they had hunted happily for grubs and centipedes.

Behind him, silent, Mud had laid out his precious Moonstones, glancing up to check the position of the sun before studying them. Thorn loped to the exposed roots of an acacia and hunkered down in its shade; this tree, he was fairly sure, was one where he and Berry had never taken shelter. He almost expected her to call up softly from the shadows below, her voice brimming with excitement.

But she would never do that again; he would never hear her voice. They had only recently been able to reveal their love to the world, after years of meeting in secret, and now their open happiness had been snatched from them in the cruelest way possible. They had had their problems and disagreements in recent moons, but Thorn knew that they would have overcome all those. Now they would never have the chance.

Foliage rustled nearby, and Spider's head appeared through the leaves, followed by Nut.

"What are you doing here?" said Thorn.

"We bumped into Sky and Big Talk," said Nut. "They thought that you were dead!"

"If I could swap places with Berry, I would," said Thorn mournfully.

"Enough of that," scolded Nut. "Both lions and elephants need you to be a Great Father now. And we are here to help you."

Thorn nodded. *I need all the friends I can get.*

Nut caught sight of Mud, muttering over the scattered Moonstones.

"Let me guess: The message isn't clear?"

Mud treated him to a scornful look. "Actually, they are," he said. He moved his fingers, gesturing in some strange pattern between the stones. "To defeat his enemy, Thorn must know him first."

"Ha!" said Nut. "*Perfectly* clear. What's that supposed to mean? Go for a walk together?"

"I think I understand," said Thorn. "There are other ways to know someone." Without explaining further, he clambered up into the crook of a trunk. Here it was shady. He closed his eyes, and as the heat of the sun faded from his fur, so he let his mind empty.

"Spider's hungry," complained the baboon below.

Thorn's eyes snapped open in exasperation, and he took a breath to scold Spider, but Mud got there first.

"Spider, be quiet," he said severely. "Thorn needs to focus. He's trying to find Titan."

Locating the lion with his mind had never been easy, but Thorn was patient. Titan was there somewhere, he had to be. But as before, his presence was blurred and obscured by the spirits of the creatures he'd consumed. Thorn vividly remembered the shock he'd felt when he'd first sensed so many hearts, so many spirits in a single place. Titan had consumed and absorbed them all, until his own self was drowning in them.

And Titan's self hadn't been a benevolent one to begin with. The madness that had taken hold of the lion only masked a deep-seated malice within his heart. Even if his reaching mind could locate Titan, Thorn knew from experience that melding with his presence would be a horrible and dark experience.

But it had to be done. Brushing aside his hesitation and his fears, Thorn gritted his jaws and let his mind drift. He

reached out farther, finding life all over Bravelands, making
the leaps he had to make.

He was a zebra, hemmed in by his herd, lazily chewing
dry yellow grass. He was a gerenuk, his delicate front hooves
planted against a tree as he reached for its softest leaves. Above
him a buzzard soared; now he was the buzzard, his keen eyes
finding movement on the plains below him. Something down
there rustled and stirred the grass, and suddenly Thorn was
the mouse that scuttled between the stems, ducking and
trembling as the buzzard's shadow passed over it.

Something huge loomed over him, something that smelled
rank and dangerous, but he was too small to catch its notice.
Thorn made the leap, finding the hyena's mind, running with
it alongside its clan as they trotted toward the Dead Forest.

But as those pale and eerie trunks rose higher in his vision,
the whole pack veered away. He turned with them, skirting
the pallid trees at a wide angle; it was for the best, because
evil lived in that forest. He was glad to follow the clan, glad to
steer clear of the ghostly trees—

No. He was Great Father Thorn, and he had a job to do.
Thorn released his hold on the hyena and soared among the
trees on the wings of a solitary weaver bird . . .

There!

Not a single, clear spirit, but a dark massing presence, a
chaos of warring existences all focused on one spot among the
pale trunks.

Titan!

Thorn did not want to approach that mass of spirits, but

he knew he must. With a sense of awful dread and reluctance, he let his mind float free of the weaver bird and sink into the morass that was Titan.

The pain and distress were even worse than he had expected. There was such sorrow here, and anger, and grief, and despite the crowding of spirits, a terrible black loneliness. He could not see through Titan's eyes; the world around him was blurred and confused, and a multitude of voices seemed to scream at him for help and for comfort. Dizzy, Thorn reeled. He clutched for purchase inside this terrible mind, but there was none: it was like trying to keep his balance on a log that rolled and bounced downstream in a raging torrent.

He had to cling on, had to know Titan's mind and his intentions. But it wasn't possible. He couldn't hold on, he would fall and drown, he—

With a stomach-churning jolt, Thorn's eyes snapped wide, and he gasped. He was back in his own body, the heat of the ravine beating down on him, and his friends were holding him.

"Thorn, are you all right?" said Mud.

"You fell from the tree!" said Nut. "It's lucky we caught you!"

"I'm fine," said Thorn, but his voice sounded thick and sluggish, and his ears rang. His limbs felt weak. Sure enough, he was at the base of the trunk where he had been sitting a moment ago.

"Thorn-friend, don't talk," cooed Spider, his voice full of concern.

"Rest for a moment," urged Nut.

"I can't!" Thorn cried in exasperation. His strength returned, and he thumped his fists on the hard ground. "I couldn't get a grip on Titan's mind at all. It's so full of other spirits, I can't focus on *him*. And it doesn't help that—that I think he's gone completely insane. I don't think any mind could cope with all those other presences."

"He was a mad lion to begin with." Nut shrugged.

"What am I going to do?" exclaimed Thorn. "I can't just go up against Titan if I don't know what he's planning. We have enough disadvantages as it is."

"Maybe you don't need to know his mind," said Mud thoughtfully.

"What? But that's the whole point—"

"No, Thorn, wait. I was thinking." Mud furrowed his brow. "What if you could get into the mind of a lion *near* Titan? One who's always with him. What about that annoying cub of his?"

Thorn blinked, startled. Now that Mud said it, it seemed obvious. "Menace?"

"That's the one." Mud nodded.

"The small, evil brute," observed Nut. "Yes, you could spy on Titan from inside her head."

"Spider thinks Mud-friend makes a good point." Spider scratched his armpit, dislodging his pet agama lizard, which scuttled indignantly onto his shoulder.

"I think so too." For the first time in what seemed an age, Thorn felt rising excitement. He closed his eyes yet again, calming his thoughts, and pictured the arrogant little lion cub. *She'll be near him. She's bound to be. I can find Titan one more time, even if I never want my mind to touch his ever again.*

A giraffe this time. That same gerenuk. One of a flock of blue starlings, massing on the grassland near the Dead Forest. A single golden wolf, trotting purposefully toward the lifeless trees—

And there was the terrible dark presence, and a smaller, more innocent one at its side. Homing in on Menace with the speed of a stooping eagle, Thorn burst into her young mind.

Compared to her father, it was almost restful to inhabit Menace's existence. This mind, Thorn realized, was arrogant, rank with a sense of entitlement, but there was a freshness and openness to it that seemed completely alien to Titan's blackly clouded presence. The cub had a meanness in her heart, but that wasn't all there was.

He was Menace, and he was thoroughly enjoying the tatters of flesh that he licked from the bone between his paws. Though he was simply a passenger in her head, her thoughts reached him along with other sensations. *Thigh of a gazelle*, her mind told him. *Delicious, and better than anything the wolves got. But then, I deserve it.*

At the thought of the wolves, Thorn-Menace glanced up at them, mouth full of warm meat. They were watching her, just a little too closely, their yellow eyes bright and hungry. A little shiver went through her spine, but she shook it off.

"Father," she said imperiously.

"What?" Titan sounded irritated, as if he'd like to flick her away with his tail like an annoying fly.

Menace wasn't put off. "Father, what's it like? Having the Great Spirit inside you?"

"What, cub?" Titan turned, his gaze impenetrable and glittering.

"What's it *feel* like?" she pressed him. "Do you feel unbeatable? Or is it all nonsense?"

Titan stretched, clawing the earth. "To be honest, the mighty Great Parent was a little disappointing." He laughed, a bone-freezing sound. "Much like any other heart. A little chewy."

"Oh." Menace's ears drooped, then perked up again. "Father, when can I start eating hearts?"

"I'll tell you what, cub." Titan prowled close and bent his head to hers. His breath was rank with blood. "When I kill Fearless, I'll let you have a bite of his. I daresay it'll be soft enough for small teeth."

Menace giggled, licking her father's nose—*Ugh*, thought Thorn, recoiling inside her—and then grew thoughtful. "Why didn't you do it then, Father? Why didn't you kill stupid Fearless when you had the chance?"

"Are you . . . *questioning* me, daughter?" Titan's eyes flashed with scorn.

"No, I—"

"Never mind. I'll tell you anyway." Titan's red tongue came out to lick his jaws. "Some hearts are better savored, young one. Fearless is an arrogant cub. He's full of himself, full of his own potential, completely certain of his sunlit future. The stronger he grows, the more full of hope and desire and eagerness, the better his heart will taste."

"Fearless is already powerful," snarled one of the wolves, padding in a circle around Titan and Menace. "That lion has killed several of the Bloodheart Pack."

"You are nothing but wolves, Maul," sneered Titan. "That's no achievement for Fearless."

Maul's hackles rose, and his muzzle peeled back to reveal his fangs. "And when will you prove *your* power, Titan? When will you deliver what you promised us?"

"Patience!" roared Titan. He lashed out with a paw, and the wolf Maul flinched back, still snarling. "You'll have what you desire, all of you. Bravelands is close to turmoil and chaos. Its creatures are weak and scattered and disoriented, and they'll cling like leeches to any leader who offers them safety and certainty. Fear begets power, Maul, don't you know that yet?"

"Oh, we know it," hissed Maul.

"Then remember it." Titan drew himself up, and his shadow seemed to fall far more broadly than it should. "Things are falling apart, and when that happens, the Bravelands herds will call one of their Great Gatherings. It's all they know, the stupid, panic-stricken fools. When the Gathering happens, *that* will be the time to explain the new order to them. And do you know what will happen?"

Maul shook his head.

"They'll welcome it," growled Titan. "They'll seize their new beginning with desperation and devotion. By that time, they'll have had more than enough of the old and dying ways."

He turned and gazed deeply into Menace's eyes. She did not move a muscle.

No. He wasn't looking into Menace's eyes. He was looking *through them*—

As if he could see what, and who, lay beyond—

"Ah, my friends, my comrades," murmured Titan, narrowing his own gaze with hateful curiosity, "someone is watching us. . . ."

"What?" exclaimed Menace. "Who, Father? Who would dare?"

"Who indeed." Titan paced closer, his muzzle lowering to his cub's, his black eyes intensely brilliant as they stared into hers. "Someone who is afraid . . ."

Thorn jerked himself violently from Menace's head. There was no time to leap from animal to animal; all he could do was let himself be snapped back through space with dizzying speed, and when he collided with his own body, he almost fainted. Staggering, he caught hold of Nut's arm and swayed, the ravine spinning around him.

Nut and Mud caught him, propping him upright, and peered at him with alarm.

"Thorn, what? What happened?" demanded Nut.

Thorn couldn't speak. *How could he see me? How? Was it one of the spirits Titan had devoured—a vulture, perhaps? He could have killed Windrider and taken her heart, and I don't think I'd know it.*

He realized he was gasping for breath. Thorn raised his eyes to those of his friends.

"Titan does have plans," he panted. "A Great Gathering—but something will happen there, something terrible. *I don't know.* I couldn't stay longer, he—"

"Thorn!" A trumpet of greeting sounded from the rim of the ravine, and he jerked his head around, startled.

An elephant gazed down at him, her ears flapping forward, her eyes warm with pleasure. "Sky Strider," he called, his voice shaky.

Behind her stood her dark-hided life-mate, Rock, and at her feet were the young cheetahs Nimble and Lively.

Weakly, Thorn gestured toward the northern end of the ravine. "There's a way down there," he called. "You and Rock can negotiate the path, I think."

"Spider will help them find the way," said Spider eagerly, and scuttled off to meet the elephants. The cheetah cubs simply bounded and leaped down the sides of the ravine, sure-footed and confident.

Nimble and Lively had already sniffed thoroughly at Nut and Mud and Thorn, had grown bored, and had withdrawn for a half-hearted play-fight by the time Spider led the elephants along the shallow stony track from the north end. Sky raised her trunk in greeting to the other three baboons.

"I can't tell you how good it is to see you, Great Father," she told Thorn softly, as Rock nodded to Nut and Mud. "We feared for a time that you were dead!"

"I should be." Thorn felt his heart sink with grief again. "It was meant to be me, Sky: I was supposed to die. Not Berry."

"Oh, Thorn." Sky curled her trunk around his shoulders and embraced him closely. "I'm so sorry. I know—we all know—how much she meant to you."

For a moment they hugged, not speaking, wrapped in their shared sadness. Then Thorn drew away, his solemn stare fixed on Sky.

"I will never stop grieving her," he said quietly. "But all I can do now is avenge her and undo the harm that has come to Bravelands. She tried to stop it, and I owe it to her to go on fighting. Or die trying."

"You won't die," said Sky fiercely. "With the help of the Great Spirit we'll defeat this evil, Thorn."

"It won't be easy," he murmured, feeling a ripple of dread chill his heart. "I've seen a little of what Titan wants to do."

"Thorn used his powers," Mud put in proudly.

"That can't have been easy," remarked Rock, and Sky nodded in agreement.

"It wasn't," admitted Thorn, "and I wish I *didn't* know. Because I don't know *enough*. All that's clear is that Titan expects us to call a Great Gathering—and that will be his opportunity to move."

"Then you can't call one," said Sky decisively. "Doing what Titan wants *must* be a bad idea."

"Maybe we don't have to, Sky. I've had a little time to think about this, and I'm the only one of us who has seen something of his mind." Thorn picked thoughtfully at a tick on his arm and frowned. "There's huge power in him, but there's madness, too, and he isn't thinking clearly or well. He's overconfident."

"He's got a right to be, by the sound of it," remarked Nut.

"But I think we can use that cockiness against him," said Thorn firmly. "Sky—I think we *should* call a Great Gathering. We can make it a trap for Titan—a counter-ambush; force him to show his schemes."

Sky swung her trunk in agitation. She cast a desperate look at Rock, then stared back at Thorn. "You're the Great Father, and I trust your wisdom, Thorn. But if a Great Gathering is exactly what Titan wants, why should we give it to him?"

"I have a plan," said Thorn, "or the beginnings of one. Berry made Titan believe she was the Great Parent, but he will know soon that he was tricked. We must spread the word that I am afraid to show my face, that I've fled Bravelands altogether. Then we call a Gathering, to announce a new Great Parent. . . ."

"And then what?" said Nut, throwing up his paws. "You'll fight him in a duel?"

"Not exactly," said Thorn. "There might be another way." The baboons looked unsure. "You must trust me. Trust the Great Spirit."

"Nimble and Lively can help carry the news of your cowardice," said Sky, her voice brimming with eagerness. The two young cheetahs raised their heads expectantly, their eyes lighting up. "They can move very quickly, can't you, cubs? And they can go almost undetected. They'll be good messengers."

"Sounds fun," said Nimble, trotting up to her.

Thorn felt possessed by a new sense of purpose. Shaking aside the grief, he bounded up onto a rock and craned his head back to gaze into the sky. There were dark flecks wheeling there, a whole flock of starlings; and two bee-eaters zipped busily across the mouth of the ravine.

Urgently Thorn clapped his paws together and let out a high-pitched hoot of summons. The others watched, fascinated, as he called over and over to the birds. They didn't know what he was saying, but it didn't matter. It was the starlings and the bee-eaters who had to understand him.

"Feather-flash, blue-streaks, whistlers!" he whooped, clear and loud. "Come, wind-soarers, sharp-wings! I summon you!"

The birds' response was instant; they circled and dived, and the distant spatter of dots in the sky swooped down so fast, they were a sudden riot of wings around Thorn. He heard gasps and cries of astonishment from Mud, Nut, and Spider, but he focused only on the birds.

Thorn could feel the light breath of their wingbeats against his fur. The bee-eaters darted to him through the cloud of starlings, like tiny colorful lightning bolts, yet not one bird so much as touched a wingtip to another's. Now Thorn could barely make out his friends; he was surrounded by beating feathers and color and fast darting movement.

"Thorn Greatfather! Thorn Greatfather! What do you need? Just ask!"

"My friends, Bravelands faces great peril," said Thorn. "All creatures must come together. Go now, fly hard and far—tell those who tread the ground that they must come to the watering hole by the light of tomorrow's dawn."

"A Great Gathering! A Great Gathering!" The cry

resounded from bird to bird, and as they spiraled up into the blue arc of sky, Thorn was left alone again, craning up on a white rock to watch them fly out of sight.

Nut, Mud, and Spider hurried back to his side, and the elephants flapped their ears in excitement. Thorn turned to them all, hope blazing aside him. *At least we are doing something*, he thought.

He rose up onto his hind paws, peeled back his muzzle, and whooped out a battle cry.

"My friends. It's time to take the fight to Titan!"

CHAPTER EIGHT

The grass was tall, and sunlight sparkled through it, dappling Swiftcub's vision. He blinked and batted a paw at a grasshopper, but it sprang away; unconcerned, Swiftcub bounded to catch up with his fathers. Gallant and Loyal padded side by side, the sun making their coats glow golden. Swiftcub gamboled between the two grown lions, and they both smiled down at him before returning to their conversation.

Swiftcub lifted his head and tail and pranced along, imagining how it must feel to be so big. One day he'd be just like them, he knew it: a tawny-maned pride leader, strong and magnificent. Why, he was almost that now. Setting his jaw, he picked up his pace, keeping up with his fathers.

But their legs were so long, their haunches so powerful. Maybe they didn't mean to, but they were speeding up, drawing away. Panting, Swiftcub trotted faster and then began to run, his short legs aching with the effort. Stop, he wanted to shout. Stop, wait for me!

But the words wouldn't come, and Gallant and Loyal became more *distant. Their silhouettes shrank into the wobbling heat haze, and Swiftcub could not keep up, no matter how fast his small paws pounded. The two lions dwindled to golden smears on the horizon, and then they vanished.*

Fearless woke with a start. An old ache of grief tugged at his heart, and he shook his head to dislodge the last traces of the dream. What did it mean?

Around him sprawled the Mightypride lions, their muzzles still bloody, their coats already sleeker in the dawn light. A lioness swatted lazily at the flies that swarmed her red-stained face; Fearless remembered her in the night, shoving her head into an antelope's belly, right down to her ears. Resolute rolled over and gave a grunting yawn of satisfaction. Three cubs lay in a haphazard pile of contentment, their flanks distended with meat.

The hunts Fearless had organized had been more than successful: a zebra and two gazelles had been brought down. There were no more growls of hostility from Mightypride; they and the Fearlesspride lions lounged together in the shade, so fully fed they were barely capable of moving. The Valorcubs suckled noisily at their mother's belly, and Mighty watched them with sleepy satisfaction.

"I dreamed I was a cub again," Fearless murmured.

"Did you?" Mighty yawned. "A strange sort of dream."

Fearless hesitated, unsure how much he wanted to talk about it. "I was with Gallant and Loyal. I suppose it was a good dream. To start with. Then I tried to keep up with them, but they left me behind."

"Of course they did." Mighty was in a much better mood,

almost back to his old self. "They're dead. You should be *grateful* they left without you." He gave a huffing laugh.

"That's a fair point," muttered Fearless.

"I knew Loyal Prideless," mused Mighty, stretching to claw the grass.

"You did?"

"We hunted together for a season, he and I." Mighty settled back to the ground. "He never talked much about himself. He was good company, but a hard lion to get to know."

"That's true," growled Fearless. *I hunted with him, talked with him, relied on him, and still he managed to hide our true relationship from me. . . .*

"I suppose Loyal had his reasons," said Mighty. "He did once let slip that he'd loved and lost, that he had a cub somewhere on the savannah, a cub he missed very much. He longed to see it, but I don't know if he ever got the chance."

"He did," said Fearless. "That was me. It was my mother Swift he loved."

"Is that so?" Mighty flicked his ears forward, startled. Then, pensively, he nodded. "So that was the connection between you? Valor didn't tell me that."

"She didn't know till recently. Neither of us did." Fearless took a breath. "I didn't find out till too late. But he knew." *At least I gave him that. . . .*

"You know how that lion broke his tail?" Mighty laughed at the memory. "We got in a fight with an entire hyena clan. I wanted to cut our losses and run, but not Loyal. *That bushbuck's ours*, he said, *and I'm not letting it go without a fight.* Well, we did have to let it go, in the end. But it certainly wasn't without a fight."

"That's . . . good to know. Thanks for telling me." Fearless grunted with amusement. "Is that how Loyal got the scar on his face too?"

Mighty nodded. "A particularly big female. Tongue-ripper, her name was. Loyal gave her some scars in exchange, though. Say, I thought Gallant was your father?"

"He was," said Fearless firmly. "They both were. I guess I'm lucky that way: two sires. Loyal was my blood father, but Gallant raised me as his own. I just hope I can live up to their memories."

Mighty looked at him, a light breeze stirring his mane. "You already are. You're a fine cub, Fearless."

It was a compliment, Fearless knew, but he felt an itch of resentment in his gut. *I'm not a cub anymore!*

But the big lion had meant well. Fearless hated to risk breaking Mighty's mood, but he still needed his help, and there seemed no better time to bring it up. "Mighty . . . about Titan . . ."

"Did someone mention Titan?" Valor rose to her paws, left her cubs, and stalked over, glaring at Fearless. "It's a pleasant morning. Let's not spoil it."

"We must speak of him," said Fearless.

Keen, lying nearby, flicked his ears toward them; then he too rose and walked across to join the little group. He said nothing, but he glanced with anxiety from Valor to Mighty to Fearless.

"Mighty, I don't want to anger you again," said Fearless, swallowing as he watched the lion's thoughtful face, "but Titan has to be confronted."

"Not anytime soon, he doesn't," snapped Valor. "I told you, it's a bright morning. Don't let your obsession ruin it."

"It's as good a moment as any," replied Fearless. "It's not just personal, Valor. You know as well as I do—no lion is safe from Titan." He flicked a worried glance at her cubs.

Valor sighed deeply and flattened her ears. She scowled. "Well, you have to make your own decisions, brother. But you don't have to drag Mighty into this." Valor's demeanor had changed subtly; she gave him a pleading look.

"Let me speak for myself, Valor," said Mighty gently. "Listen, Fearless, I spoke to many of your pride last night, and I listened to what they had to say about Titan. Especially the ones who were in Titanpride—they knew him best. And I can't deny that what they told me was alarming. This heart-eating business—it disturbs me. But we've all eaten hearts, Fearless."

"But this is different," urged Fearless. "Titan takes the heart before his victim's spirit can leave for the stars. It's a trick of the golden wolves, an evil tradition. No lion should kill in such a way—and Titan takes *only* the hearts."

"Well, it *is* Codebreaking, but that's nothing new from Titan." Mighty licked his jaws and made a face.

"Mighty! *Mighty!*" A young lion bounded up, skidding to a halt so fast he kicked up a cloud of dust. "You have to come!"

Mighty turned to him. "What is it, Noble? You're supposed to be scouting—"

"That's exactly what I'm doing," said Noble. "And Titan Wolfpride has just marched straight into your territory!"

"What?" Mighty leaped to his feet.

Fearless sprang up beside him, his fangs bared. "I have to fight Titan!"

"No," snarled Mighty, shaking his mane. "This is my territory, Fearless. I'll see this intruder off!"

"You don't understand!" exclaimed Fearless, his eyes widening. "Titan's a cheat and a murderer. He doesn't fight fair."

"Yes, so I've heard," said Mighty with a glance at Valor. "Noble, are Titan's wolves with him?"

"Not that we could see, Mighty. He's come alone." Noble growled. "The insolence!"

"Then, Fearless, you have nothing to worry about. I will deal with this arrogant lion, and I'll do it alone." Mighty's muzzle wrinkled in anger.

"But—" Fearless began.

Then he caught the look Keen gave him, and the slight shake of his head.

No, he thought. *Keen's right. I'm a guest on Mightypride territory.* And the great lion had treated him with generosity and patience; Fearless had no right to quarrel with him. He dipped his head. "Be careful, Mighty," he muttered.

"That will hardly be necessary," growled Mighty with amusement. "But nevertheless, I'll bear your advice in mind."

Tossing his mane and squaring his shoulders, Mighty strode off after Noble. Fearless, Keen, Valor, and the rest of the pride fell in behind the leader, ears, tails, and whiskers twitching with anticipation.

Titan came into view far too soon, pacing briskly across the plain toward Mighty. The two huge lions halted when they were a gazelle-spring apart, their blazing eyes locked on each other. For a terrible moment, there was nothing but taut silence. The air shimmered with heat. Then the eerie cry of an eagle overhead split the air.

Titan slammed a paw against the ground, raking his claws through the dust. His muzzle peeled back from bloody fangs.

"There you stand, Mighty Mightypride. I, Titan of Wolf-pride, come to claim your heart."

A shudder of dread went through Fearless: the words were a twisted version of the traditional lion challenge. He shot a look at Keen, and what he saw in his friend's eyes did not reassure him: it was fear. Keen swallowed, but his stare hardened and he stood up straighter beside Valor. All of Mightypride glared in defiant hostility at the massive, black-maned intruder.

There was amusement beneath the anger in Mighty's voice.

"And I, Mighty, fight to keep . . . my heart."

For a moment, though, the lions did not move. Titan's dark gaze slid toward Fearless.

"Ah, there you are, Gallantbrat. Shouldn't you be standing in Mighty's place at this moment? There was . . . oh, let me try to remember . . . an oath, wasn't there? So why is Mighty fighting your battles for you?"

Fearless gave a growl of anger, deep in his throat. The muscles of his stiff forelegs trembled, and his hide prickled all over with loathing.

But he glanced at Mighty and dipped his head in respect. "Because, Titan, this isn't my battle. Not right here and now."

"An oath-breaker, then: just like your father Loyal *Prideless.*" Titan spat the words.

Every bone and muscle in Fearless's body itched to launch himself at his sneering enemy, but Mighty's presence held him back. He could not disrespect the lion in his own territory, no matter how badly he wanted to claw Titan's glittering eyes from his skull.

He could only snarl in frustration and force his trembling paws into stillness, as Mighty and Titan began to circle each other, their eyes locked. *But I am supposed to kill Titan. Me!*

"Mighty is a great hunter," Valor whispered next to him. "If anyone can defeat Titan, it's him."

Fearless nudged her with his head, trying to push down his own disappointment. "I know," he said quietly, but inside he was thinking something else. *Fighting isn't the same thing as hunting.*

There was no more time for talk. Bunching their rippling muscles, the two lions roared and sprang into violent combat.

The ground seemed to shake beneath Fearless's paws. Both lions were huge, and Titan's fury and hatred seemed to shimmer around him like the heat on the horizon. But Mighty was no easy opponent, and his calm determination was an advantage. Where Titan clawed and lashed and flung himself wildly, Mighty took the time to dodge and position himself, aiming well-placed blows at his enemy. Titan gave a high-pitched snarl of frustration as his claws missed their mark yet again, and Mighty's huge paw slammed him to the ground.

Titan rolled and struggled to his feet, his flanks heaving with rage. Exposing his fangs, he launched himself at Mighty's throat; Mighty ducked, spun, and, as Titan stumbled and slid, rose up, raking his long claws across Titan's shoulder. An arc of blood sprayed, and one of the Mightypride cubs whimpered in fear.

Titan sprang up yet again, but he was growing tired, and he staggered. Mighty pressed his advantage. Eyes gleaming, he flung himself at his opponent, sinking his jaws into Titan's shoulder blade. Titan howled with pain and rolled, but Mighty did not loosen his grip. His claws lodged deep into Titan's flanks and as the black-maned lion struggled and kicked, he held him down with his massive weight.

Paws scrabbling, Titan gave a despairing snarl of fury. "I yield!"

"You what?" Mighty's growl was muffled by a jawful of black mane.

"I *yield!*" roared Titan.

With a last hard swipe at his skull, Mighty released Titan and stepped back.

Fearless's heart soared. Not only had Mighty won a noble and fair victory, he had accepted Titan's surrender, in full view of his pride. Titan would live another day—and he was still Fearless's to kill.

"Get off my territory," growled Mighty to Titan, loud and clear. "Come back here, and you die."

The black-maned lion flinched, glaring up at Mighty as he turned his rump and strode back to his pride. Fearless felt a fierce glow of triumph to see Titan beaten and cowed, head lowered in defeat—

Titan glanced up. In his eyes, spiteful glee flared. *He's acting!* realized Fearless.

He roared a horrified warning. "Mighty, *no!* It's a trick!"

But Titan had already moved, faster than Fearless would have believed possible. With the sudden speed and agility of a cheetah, he was on Mighty. Sinuous and powerful as a crocodile, he dragged the golden-maned lion down, rolling him, and his jaws opened wide.

Fearless barely had time to register the startled astonishment in Mighty's eyes. The big lion didn't even have time for fear. The jaws snapped and tore into his throat with the brutal efficiency of the croc-spirit inside Titan.

Blood spurted bright red in the sunlight. And Mighty collapsed to the earth with a sound like thunder, his life already draining, a dark and spreading stain on the yellow sand.

CHAPTER NINE

The bright, hot air of the savannah seemed motionless; like everything and everyone, silent with shock. For long moments, Fearless could hear not so much as the cry of a bird or the scratch of an insect. And then, the terrible stillness was shattered.

"NO!" Valor's roar of grief resounded across the grassland. She sprang forward, the Valorcubs stumbling after her in bewilderment. A little way from Mighty's body, Valor halted, her flanks heaving as she stared down at her lifeless mate.

"Mother?" squeaked the bolder Valorcub, flattening his ears in confusion. His shyer brother sidled to press against him, and both cubs blinked up in bewilderment at Valor.

"Is Father sleeping?" asked the timid cub.

Valor didn't look down at them. Her whiskers bristled as she stared wide-eyed at Mighty, and her muzzle twisted with grief and fury. Fearless recalled the moment, as a slightly older cub himself, that he'd watched Gallant be killed.

The lions of Mightypride stalked to Valor's side, gathering protectively around the grieving lioness. They growled, glaring their hatred at the victorious Titan. He, though, was not intimidated; he tossed his black mane, with a horrible grunting laugh that was almost crocodilian.

Heart thundering with anger, Fearless bounded to stand at their head, his eyes fixed on his enemy. Keen raced to his flank.

"You cheat and lie and play tricks, Titan Wolfpride," snarled Fearless. "*Again.* You were beaten in fair combat. Mighty defeated you!"

Titan stood very still, studying the lions of Mightypride with cold amusement. His eyes slid to Mighty's corpse.

"It doesn't look like that to me," he growled. His gaze flicked up again to survey the furious lions. "And now you are all Titanpride. You serve *me.*"

"Never," roared Keen, striking the earth with his claws. "I speak for all of Mightypride when I tell you this: we will never follow you, Titan."

"You won't have to, Keen," snarled Fearless. He took a bounding leap forward, so that he was glaring at Titan over the body of Mighty. "None of you even have time to become Titanpride. Because I'll kill this evil, cheating coward, here and now!"

His muscles bunched and tightened, and his claws sprang from their sheaths. Exposing his fangs fully, he let out a roar that shook the plain. His own blood pounded in his ears.

And then, as he was about to leap at the tyrant, to put an end to him once and for all, he heard Keen's warning cry resonate in the clear air.

"Wolves! Beware!"

Fearless turned his head from side to side, staring at the oncoming wolf pack. They came slowly, tongues lolling, their yellow eyes bright with glee. Spreading out, the wolves circled the lions of Mightypride, hemming them in.

Fearless caught Titan's dark gaze, one last time. It was filled with contempt and scorn.

"Not today, Gallantbrat," growled the black-maned lion. "Pride! Attack!"

The wolves rushed in, and Fearless spun to roar at Mightypride.

"Protect the cubs! Protect Valor!"

The Mightypride lions needed no urging. Already some of the lionesses were shepherding the youngsters away, to cower in the grass beneath the trees or shelter behind boulders. Other lionesses and young males advanced to meet the advancing wolves.

Red dust billowed up from the earth from the mass of frantic paws. The odds were in the lions' favor, even though they were outnumbered five to one. But still Fearless felt a tremor of panic. The wolves became a mob of glittering eyes and teeth, drool flying from their jaws as they sprang. Snarling, the lions collided with them in a flurry of claws and fangs.

Fearless was almost blinded by the dust, but he lashed and

snapped instinctively, spinning to snatch a wolf by its scrawny neck, shaking off another as soon as he felt its claws scrape his rump. He heard Keen give a roar of fury, and out of the dust cloud a wolf was flung at his forepaws, limp and glassy-eyed, its blood trickling into the earth. Fearless dodged, leaped over its corpse, and tore another wolf away from Glory's rump. She twisted and seized its foreleg in her jaws as Fearless tore at its haunch, and between them they ripped it apart. Fearless did not pause to enjoy one small victory; he bounded over the wolf's shattered body and sprang at another.

The wolves—fueled by the spirits and strength of so many of their victims—seemed undeterred by the slaughter of their pack-mates. Wave after wave surged at the Mightypride lions, and despite the lions' superior strength and size, Fearless realized they were being forced relentlessly back toward the acacias where the cubs sheltered. And it did not seem to matter how many wolves were thrown aside, dead or wounded; more of them rushed on, eager and slavering, taking the places of their dead comrades without, it seemed, a concern for their own lives.

"They're trying to get the cubs!" panted Keen, as he snatched a moment beside Fearless to gather his breath.

Fearless had no time to reply; four more wolves were bolting toward them. But he knew Keen was right. It was customary for a new pride leader to kill his predecessor's cubs; that was the way of lions. But to send these mad wolves to do it for him? Titan was completely heedless of honor or even of the most bloodthirsty traditions.

The Mightypride lions were fighting a battle for the future of their pride, though; and slowly, wolf by beaten wolf, they were gaining the upper paw. As the dust thinned and the noise of yelping and roaring subsided, Fearless realized that it was, quite suddenly, over. A few remaining wolves turned tail and fled, many of them limping or dragging their haunches; those would die soon, he knew, killed and eaten by their own pack. Wolf corpses littered the dry ground, which was stained dark with patches of blood. Many lions—himself included—bore bites and deep scratches, but no lions had died today.

Except for one. Fearless, panting for breath, padded over to where Mighty's body lay. Valor had reached it before him; she crouched at her mate's side, her head pressed to his shoulder. Titan was nowhere to be seen. But a new ragged wound had been ripped in Mighty's chest, and Fearless saw that his heart had been torn from him. His own heart lurched within him.

"It can't be true," Valor was muttering as Fearless came to her side. "It can't. It's too wrong. His heart, Fearless."

Crouching beside his sister, Fearless licked gently at her ear. "I'm so sorry, Valor."

"He can't be dead. He was with me just this morning. This *morning*."

"Your cubs, Valor?" he asked urgently.

She jerked her head back at the acacias. "They're safe. With Gentle. Oh, Fearless, how can I protect them now? Their father is *dead*."

"Our father died," he reminded her gently. "We survived, Valor, and your cubs too will learn to be strong and fierce and honorable. Just like Mighty."

"How could he be so stupid?" She sat suddenly back on her haunches. "This was always going to happen! I warned him! You warned him! Titan always wins!"

"Don't be angry, Valor," Fearless growled softly. "He had no choice. You know that. This was Titan's doing, not Mighty's."

Valor's head sagged again. "Yes. Titan. There's no peace, no safety while Titan lives: not for any creature. Oh, Mighty-pride should have left Bravelands long ago, found a new home far from that mad savage. What will we do now?"

"This is your fault!" Glory snarled behind Fearless. "You led Titan here!"

Fearless twisted to face her, shocked. "No, Glory. Titan *always* planned to come here."

"Looking for *you*! If you hadn't arrived, Mighty would not be dead!"

Fearless stared at her, his throat constricting. He wanted to deny it, wanted to argue. But somewhere inside him, he had a dreadful suspicion that Glory spoke the truth.

"No." Keen walked forward to stand between them, his brown eyes intent on the lioness. "It's not true, Glory. Fearless came here to warn Mighty, and he was right. Titan isn't looking only to kill Fearless. He came here to strengthen himself by taking out a powerful pride leader. He would have come for Mighty eventually, whatever happened."

Glory glowered at him for a moment, but at last she gave a reluctant nod.

"I think it's true, Glory," said Valor hoarsely.

Keen glanced from one lioness to the other, then raised his head to take in all the lions of Mightypride, who were approaching one by one. Some limped; some paused to lick at wounds on their paws and flanks. One had lost an eye to a wolf's claw, but his face was still grim with defiance.

"We need to hold together now," declared Keen, his roar ringing across the plain. "If we scatter, if we fight among ourselves, Titan and his unnatural pride will pick us off one by one, like gazelles who flee the herd in panic. It's more important than ever that we true lions stay as one."

The one-eyed young lion gave a grunting roar of approval, and one by one the others joined him.

Valor, though, remained at Mighty's side, her head still pressed against him. Fearless felt his heart lurch with pity.

"Oh, Valor," he murmured, bending to nuzzle her head. "Mighty lived up to his name. You'll be telling the story to his cubs for many seasons. He faced down Titan, and he beat him—however it ended. He fought for you, and for them, and for his pride, and he did it with honor."

"Yes." Valor's voice was broken and muffled, and she didn't look up at him. "But still, he is dead."

A shiver of uncertainty rippled through Fearless's gut, making his fur rise. Valor had told Glory that Keen was right, that Fearless wasn't to blame. But there must be at least a small part of his sister that wondered: If Fearless hadn't shown up, if he hadn't sought out Mighty's help, would the great lion still be alive?

"Valor," he whispered, "I swear I'll protect you and your

cubs. Until you choose to leave for another pride, you're my responsibility. I'll keep you safe, I promise you."

She gave a heavy sigh as she lifted her head at last. "Can you promise that, Fearless? Can you, truly? It's *Titan*."

He felt that shiver run through his fur again. "I'll try," he whispered. "But Valor, we have to move away from this place."

"I won't leave Mighty!" She spun to face him, her eyes fiery.

Keen trotted over, his expression anxious. "Valor, you know Fearless is right. And you must leave Mighty. He will return to the earth as he should, become a part of Bravelands. You must come away and bring his cubs to a place of safety."

"Yes." Another lion padded forward; Fearless saw it was Resolute. The older lion gave him a glance that Fearless couldn't read. "And I believe we have a leader; the only lion who actually understands what is going on in Bravelands. It seems we are Fearlesspride now."

"It seems so." Keen shot Fearless a sideways look, and at last there was a spark of unmissable affection in it.

A reluctant murmur of growling agreement ran through the Mightypride lions, but Fearless shook his head and stood up, his muscles tensing.

"No, Resolute! No, Keen, I can't. I haven't earned it."

"It's not a question of earning it." Glory shrugged. "These are not normal times. Everything has changed, for now at least. I agree with Resolute. I think we all do."

Looking around at their weary, bloodied faces, Fearless nodded slowly. His heart thudded.

"All right," he growled at last. "For now, we are Fearlesspride.

But I promise you, I won't remain your leader simply because you have no choice. If I am to keep the pride leadership, I will prove myself worthy of it."

"Agreed," said Resolute, with a nod.

"Agreed," said Glory.

Keen licked Fearless's cheekbone. "Yes. I'd expect no less from you, my old friend."

At Mighty's side, Valor rose to her paws. She gazed down mournfully for long moments, then slowly turned away from her dead mate.

"Fearlesspride," she growled softly. "So that my Valorcubs might be safe, at least for now."

As the rumble of approval spread and rose around the former Mightypride, Fearless nodded at Keen.

"Thank you, Keen. For your faith in me."

Keen laughed softly. "That's never wavered, Fearless. Even when I disapprove of your vendetta. And you're right: we need to leave this place."

Fearless glanced at the sky. Already the vultures were circling, broad black wings tilting to catch the air currents as they drifted lower. In the scrub a little way distant, jackals gave nervous, high-pitched yelps of impatience.

"It's time, Valor." Fearless nudged his sister gently.

Then, with a grunting bellow of summons, he turned and strode away from the spot where Mighty's body lay. And the lions of Fearlesspride, one by one, fell in behind and followed him.

CHAPTER TEN

"*It's the oddest plan I've ever* heard, Sky," said Comet, flapping her ears.

"Is that quite true, Comet?" Boulder laughed. "Haven't you spoken with my sister at all, these last few seasons?"

Comet shot him a sharp look; then she too gave a rumble of laughter. "You're right, Boulder. It's a long time since Sky planned anything normal or traditional. Very well, Sky. For you, we'll pretend that the Great Parent is dead."

Comet and Boulder stood apart from the herds, talking in soft voices with Sky and Rock. Some distance away, a vast mass of elephants lingered on the pale and dusty plain, males and females all intermingled. Calves played together, blowing at the dust and chasing rats and guinea fowl; the adults watched them with keen, amused gazes. A bull flapped his ears in warning at a buffalo herd that wandered too close, and for a few moments he and the chief buffalo glared indignantly at each other, before drifting apart with nods of respect.

Sky found that she was happy to be back with the herds, watching their daily routine and living it with them. When she and Rock had trudged back to rejoin the other elephants, it had felt like the most natural thing in the world. Perhaps her days of wandering alone were almost over? One day soon the male and female herds would separate and go their own ways, Sky was aware; but even that knowledge didn't dismay her as it might once have done. She was betrothed to Rock, and they had renewed their vows to each other. They would always find each other again, as elephants did.

As if knowing her thoughts, Rock edged closer to her and hooked his trunk over hers. "We came as soon as we could to share Thorn's plan," he told Boulder and Comet. "I think it's a good one, even if nothing like it has ever been necessary before."

"I'll be so happy when life in Bravelands returns to normal." Comet rolled her eyes.

"But it won't until we defeat Titan," said Sky firmly.

"I still don't understand exactly what Thorn's plan *is*," said Boulder. "We pretend the Great Father is dead, we tell every creature we meet, we promise a new Great Parent will be along soon— but then what? What's the point of this deception?"

"I wish I could tell you, brother," murmured Sky, "but I made a promise to the Great Father. I know he can trust you, but we don't know what other animals might overhear, and we mustn't reveal the plan to Titan or his spies. Titan must go on thinking that everything is going his way, that his plans are succeeding. It's the only way we'll ever catch him off guard."

"Titan may know now that Berry was not the Great Parent," rumbled Rock softly. "If that's the case, he must be made to believe that Thorn has fled, never to return."

"So." Sky looked from Boulder to Comet and back again. "Will you trust me?"

Comet gave a sigh. "Sky Strider, you've always walked your own path. I know that, and of course I trust you. Your wildest ideas, young one, always seem to make sense in the end."

"Thank you, Comet." Sky dipped her head and butted her trunk gratefully against Comet's.

"And of course I'll go along with it," said Boulder gruffly. "If I can't trust my own crazy sister, who can I trust?"

Sky gave a rumble of laughter. "Thank you, brother."

"But really, I think the best option is the most straight-forward one," Boulder added. "If Titan comes to the Great Gathering, we simply stampede and trample him to lion-meat for the birds."

"That sounds good in theory," pointed out Rock, "but Titan's too clever for such a ploy. He'd escape somehow, and then he'd be on to us. No, Sky thinks that Thorn's plan has the greatest chance of success."

"All right, then," sighed Comet, shaking her ears. "Boulder and I will tell the elephants that the Great Father is gone. We'll make sure it spreads far and wide, with every creature we meet as we travel. And of course, we'll lead our own herds to the Great Gathering when the time comes."

Boulder nodded. "But I promise you one thing, Sky. If this plan of Thorn's fails—whatever it is—I'll stand ready to take care of Titan. He has to be stopped now, and sometimes the plainest ways are the best."

"I appreciate it," Sky told the two elephants softly, "and so does the Great Father. The Great Spirit go with you on your travels."

As the two leaders turned and trudged back toward their herds, Sky watched them with yearning. *One day soon*, she promised herself. Soon she would walk with her family again, for good.

Now, though, she had to turn away with Rock and begin the journey back to the Great Father. Together they strode away across the plain toward the thin line of dark forest in the distance.

"I didn't want to say anything in front of Comet and Boulder," remarked Rock, when the herds behind them were nothing but a smear of shimmering gray against the horizon, "but do you really think the Great Father's plan can work? It's very ambitious. I know Thorn is considered clever even among the baboons, but . . ." His voice trailed off uneasily.

"Don't worry," Sky told him firmly, touching his shoulder with her trunk. "The plan isn't just Thorn's, remember. The Great Spirit itself is working through him. And if the plan is the Great Spirit's—how can it possibly fail?"

* * *

The way seemed longer than it had when they had made the outward journey; the savannah they traveled across was featureless, dotted only with the occasional flat-topped acacia, and in the shimmering heat it was hard to judge how far they'd come and how far they still had to go. Sky's throat was dry, and she was glad of the still green waters of the river that wound lazily across the flatlands. On its muddy banks scrubby trees grew, and the two elephants halted to browse on the branches, snapping and chewing. Herds of grass-eaters shimmered in the middle distance, grazing in the glare of the high sun.

"Look at those zebras." Rock raised his head and shook his ears in amusement. "They've got more energy than I do in this heat."

Sky followed his gaze. The small zebra herd was not grazing; the animals stood in an alert circle, ears twitching and tails flicking, watching two stallions fight. The combat looked fierce and unforgiving, thought Sky: both males reared up, striking at each other with brutal determination. One swung around, lashing out with his hind hooves and catching his unwary opponent in the throat. The other staggered, backed off for a moment with flanks heaving, then flung himself back into battle. He seized the first zebra's withers in his jaws, biting and shaking. With a scream of pain and fury, his opponent shook him off and gave him a ringing blow on the side of the head.

"They're both big stallions," said Sky. She ambled closer, curious, and Rock followed. "This could go on for a while."

"What are they fighting about?" Rock asked a lanky mare

as the elephants drew close to the herd.

She flicked her tail, not taking her eyes off the battle. "Leadership of the herd, obviously," she told him distractedly.

"They're well matched," observed Sky. "So who do you think will win?"

"Can't say." The mare sounded impatient. "Always hard to judge. Silverfriend is younger and fitter, but Bristlefriend has more experience."

Sky peered, fascinated. Both zebras were catching their breath, circling each other, gazes locked in determination. With a sudden burst of energy, the younger one galloped forward, teeth bared in a scream of challenge. Bristlefriend dodged the attack. He twisted again, and this time the kick he aimed with his hind hooves caught Silverfriend right on the cheekbone. The young zebra staggered, then halted in a daze, swaying. Bristlefriend whirled and slammed his front hooves against his shoulder, and Silverfriend collapsed onto his side, flanks heaving. His whinnying groan of defeat told Sky the fight was over.

Panting, snorting, Bristlefriend backed away from the prone stallion. "You yield, friend?"

"I yield," gasped Silverfriend.

"Good." Bristlefriend nodded, tossing his stiff mane. "Hail, my herd leader!"

"Wait," whispered Sky to Rock, startled. *"What?"*

A chorus of neighs rose up from the watching herd. "Hail, herd leader Silverfriend!"

"We follow you, Silverfriend!"

"Lead us on to sweet grass."

As Bristlefriend trotted triumphantly back to the herd, Silverfriend scrambled painfully to his feet. The younger zebra's head and tail drooped; he looked utterly miserable at his new status.

Sky exchanged a bewildered look with Rock. "I don't understand. What just happened?"

Rock shook his ears slowly. "No idea. This is weird."

The short-tempered mare turned to give them both a withering look. "Don't you know? The herds have a new tradition. Bristlefriend and Silverfriend were fighting *not* to be leader."

"But . . . surely the strongest should lead?" Sky blinked in confusion.

"Of course not," snapped the mare, and the zebras around her nodded in agreement. "If you're a leader, the spirit-eating lion will come for your heart. Don't you know that? Hmph!"

Without another word, she trotted away with her friends to congratulate Bristlefriend and pay respects to the exhausted and dejected Silverfriend. Sky turned to Rock, her mind and heart in turmoil; this was all so wrong.

"Titan's behavior is causing chaos," she told Rock. "Everything is upside down and the wrong way around. This can't go on!"

"I agree," rumbled Rock, his brow furrowed in anxiety. "The strongest must lead, or the herds will dwindle and diminish. And that in turn affects every creature."

"Titan is the opposite of the Great Spirit," declared Sky. "He destroys the balance of life and brings meaningless death wherever he goes."

"All the more reason to bring these animals to the Great Gathering," Rock told her. "If you can convince them, Sky." He sighed. "When creatures have lost their way this badly, I wonder if they listen to wisdom or advice anymore?"

"I know what to do." Flapping her ears grimly, Sky marched forward to the center of the herd. Zebras backed off hurriedly as she made her way through the crowd to the doleful-looking Silverfriend. Bristlefriend stood at his side, rubbing his withers consolingly with his teeth.

"Sorry I bit so hard," he was saying. "You fought well, Silverfriend. Bad luck, really."

"No need to apologize," grunted Silverfriend. "The best zebra won."

"That's exactly the problem!" trumpeted Sky in exasperation as she came to a halt. "The best zebra should be *leading* your herd, not fighting to stay in the background."

Bristlefriend glared at her sulkily. "You don't understand."

"I understand far too well!" Sky drew a deep breath; there was no point being angry with the zebras. This was not their doing. "Listen to me, my friends. Silverfriend does not want this leadership, any more than Bristlefriend did. How well can he possibly lead you?"

"That's not what's important anymore," snapped another mare. "It's all very well for an elephant to judge. You're enormous! It's a lot harder for a pack of wolves to take *you* down.

Nobody wants to volunteer to have their heart ripped out and eaten!"

Sky dipped her head in acknowledgment of what was a perfectly fair point. Then she blinked around at the truculent zebra herd. "But you must see, all of you, that this new strategy of yours can't end well."

"It's how it has to be," pointed out Silverfriend. "There are other considerations. I accept my fate."

The other zebras nodded and murmured in admiration.

"Well, you shouldn't," Sky told him sharply. "None of us should. Titan will destroy all of Bravelands with his unnatural brutality! How will the herds thrive and prosper if the best animals do not lead them?"

"But how will they survive," whinnied Bristlefriend, "if the best animals lead them for half a day before their hearts are eaten?"

"That's why I have a proposal for you." Sky took a deep breath, waiting until all the zebras had quieted and turned to watch her expectantly. "I volunteer to be your leader. For now. I will take the risk; let Titan come for me."

Silverfriend's ears pricked forward; he looked more cheerful than he had since Sky had first laid eyes on him. "Well," he said, glancing at the herd, "she *is* an elephant."

The zebras exchanged doubtful looks.

"That's true," said a mare.

"Yes, Flickfriend!" snapped another. "An elephant! She's big and she's strong, but she's not a zebra! How can we be led by a *not-a-zebra*?"

"Just for now," Sky reminded them quickly.

"Mind you, Titan eats elephant hearts as well as—*ow!*" A young colt glared at the neighbor who had kicked him, but he shut up.

"I think it's not a bad idea," said Flickfriend the mare.

"Same here," put in another.

"I think it's a *great* idea." Silverfriend's whinny was a little too eager, and some of the mares gave him disdainful looks.

"So we're all agreed," announced Bristlefriend. "The elephant can be our leader until Titan's defeated."

Rock took a sharp inward breath. He looked as if he might say something and opened his mouth, but Sky gave him a tiny shake of her head. "Rock, I want to do this."

Sighing in resignation, he nodded. "Very well, Sky. You can still surprise me." He smiled. "But we should all be aware— there are wolves watching us."

Sky gasped, "Where?" The nearest zebras whinnied in alarm and pawed the ground.

"Don't look right at them." Rock lowered his voice. "But that escarpment just beyond the river? They're skulking behind that cluster of bigger boulders. Spying on us."

"Are they indeed?" Glancing airily around, as if she were simply fanning her ears to cool them, Sky caught a glimpse of shadows in the shimmering air by the escarpment. "Then let's give them some news to take back to Titan, shall we?"

The zebras looked at one another again. "If that's all part of your strange elephant plan." Bristlefriend shrugged, and the herd nodded.

Sky lifted her trunk and made a loud, ringing declaration.

"Be at the Great Gathering, my zebra friends," she cried. "At the watering hole a new Great Parent will come forward to lead us. He or she will do what Thorn could not, and deal with Titan Wolfpride once and for all! Let us all trust in the Great Spirit!"

The zebras whinnied with excitement, pawing the earth into a rising dust cloud, rearing up, and flailing their forefeet. Bristlefriend arched his neck and bucked with delight.

"A new Great Parent," he neighed. "We will come, Sky Strider!"

"To the watering hole!" whinnied Silverfriend.

Yes, thought Sky, *to the Great Gathering*. The skulking wolves were already moving, she noticed from the corner of her eye: sinuous shapes bounded up the escarpment and vanished into the haze. They would take the news back to Titan, and Titan would make his next move.

And Great Father Thorn's plan would be in motion. . . .

CHAPTER ELEVEN

The dusty earth was hot under Fearless's paws, the grass dry and brittle. Even though the landscape wobbled in the heat haze, he was aware of slinking golden shadows at the edge of his vision. The wolves had followed as he led his own lions and the former Mightypride in search of new territory.

So long as they kept their distance, the wolves could be ignored. And Fearless had stationed scouts at the flanks of their traveling group, so he would have plenty of warning if the wolves launched an attack, or if Titan showed up again. So far, though, the wolves had shown no signs of coming closer. They were keeping an eye on Fearlesspride, that was all, and no doubt reporting their movements back to Titan.

A sick feeling of anger churned in Fearless's gut, but the wolf-spies had to be put to the back of his mind for now. It was his growing pride that mattered, and their search for a safe home. Barely any of the lions had spoken since they had set off from Mighty's old territory; the mood of the whole pride was dark, the newcomers still grieving and angry over their leader's death.

Fearless knew exactly how they felt—after all, he'd long ago seen his own father, Gallant, murdered by Titan, with an equally vicious and sneaky trick.

Valor had witnessed that, too; and now she had seen Titan kill her beloved mate. Fearless glanced back at his sister, concerned. She trudged a little way behind, her paws pacing more by instinct than with intent. Her two tiny cubs scampered beside her, doing their best to keep up; she murmured encouragement to them, keeping their spirits up, but her own eyes seemed dull. She was still weak from birthing and nursing, Fearless realized, and now she had lost her mate and protector. *But I will never abandon her. I'll keep that promise.*

The cubs were too young to truly understand, thought Fearless, and for that he was glad. They might not have clear memories of their father in the future, but at least they would not carry such a weight of grief through their lives as he and Valor had.

"Where are we heading, Fearless?" Keen trotted to his side, his ears twitching with alertness. "I don't like the way those wolves are tracking us, but I don't think there's anything we can do while they keep their distance. If they know where we go, how can any place be safe?"

"I have an idea," Fearless told him. Halting, he lifted his head and nodded at an outcrop of rocky ground in the distance. "Loyal's old cave, in that kopje, will be the best place to hide the cubs and protect them. Yes, the wolves will see us go there—but it's on a high spot, it's easy to defend, and there's only one entrance. I'm sure we can keep enemies at bay."

"Not bad, for a temporary measure," said Keen. "All right. But it won't be secure forever."

"Titan won't live forever," growled Fearless. "I promise you that."

As the pride approached the kopje and began to scramble up the rocks toward the cavern entrance, Fearless halted, sniffing the air and scanning the savannah. The wolves were still there, sinister shapes in the grass, but they too had halted and made no move to come closer now. There were herds moving on the border of a distant forest, starlings wheeled in the sky, and a lizard scuttled away from the lions' paws, but Fearless could make out no immediate threats. There was certainly no sign of Titan.

Fearless bounded up the rocks to the small plateau in front of Loyal's old cave, and he waited there until Valor had shepherded her cubs into the cool and secure darkness within. Other lionesses and their cubs followed her, but the younger lionesses and adult males clustered around Fearless, their gazes expectant.

He swallowed, trying to look as if he was absolutely certain what he was doing. "Resolute, Glory, Noble—post guards on the plain, around the kopje. We can't allow any intruders to get through to the cubs. And a patrol would be good, farther out on the grassland. Those wolves know what we're up to;

let's give them the same close attention that they give us."

"Very well, Fearless." Resolute nodded.

"Keen, stay with me close to the cave," said Fearless. "We can keep an eye on the lionesses and the cubs. We—"

As a flock of egrets cried above him in the blue arc of the sky, he glanced up. Their flight seemed unusually purposeful, and there was an urgency and excitement to their calls that even he, a Grasstongue-speaker, could recognize.

That must be the summons for Thorn's Great Gathering. "Look, Keen: the Great Father has summoned the herds. Those are herald birds."

"Are they?" Keen looked to the sky skeptically; the egrets were already dwindling to dots over the far hills. "What's that got to do with us?"

"I need to be there," murmured Fearless. "Something important is happening."

"Important or not," put in Resolute, "it has nothing to do with lions."

"I agree," said Glory. "Your place is with your pride, Fearless."

"Especially at a time like this," added Noble, who seemed to be making an effort not to gape at Fearless as if he was mad.

"They're all quite right," Keen told Fearless firmly. "You can't go dashing off to some Great Parent business right now. You've gathered your pride—you need to protect it."

Reluctantly, Fearless nodded. "All right. I know. I just wish I could be there."

"I don't see why." Resolute shrugged. "This Great Parent

of yours seems even more pointless than he was before. What happened to the last four? All dead, as I recall, in gruesome circumstances."

"The elephant was killed by crocodiles," said Glory, "and the rhino was chased over a ridge."

"The first baboon was torn to pieces by crocs as well," added Noble.

"He was not a true Parent," snapped Fearless.

"But you thought the next baboon was. And now he's run away too." Resolute huffed in derision. "What your Great Spirit was thinking, picking baboons, I have no idea. But leave them to it, Fearless. The Spirit, if it exists, clearly has no power at all."

Fearless bit down his angry urge to roar the truth: *Thorn isn't a coward! He's one of the strongest Great Parents there has ever been, and he's our best hope!*

But that secret had to be kept safe, and there was no point arguing with his pride. Besides, in these circumstances their advice was sound. Fearless knew it, but he couldn't help a wrench of longing to join his friend Thorn, to help him in his mission to destroy Titan.

Thorn was clever, thought Fearless, but he would have to be far more than clever to outwit the powerful Titan. Only a sunset ago he'd believed Thorn dead; he didn't know if he could bear to go through that grief yet again, for real this time. And Thorn might be the Great Parent, but what the lions said was true: he was a baboon. A *vulnerable* baboon.

What are you planning, Thorn? I have a duty to my pride, but I want so much to help.

Fearless closed his eyes and begged with all the urgency he could muster. *Please, Great Spirit. Please keep my old friend safe. . . .*

Dusk fell swiftly, a violet haze that deepened to darkest blue, and the coolness was a soothing relief after the heat and flies of the day. From his position on the kopje, Fearless listened to the chirp of crickets and watched the distant horizon swallow up the last traces of the sun. Stars began to glitter and twinkle above him, and the eyes of night hunters glowed as they emerged from their daytime burrows: an aardwolf, a pair of civets, a bat-eared fox.

Even with his night vision, Fearless could no longer make out the distant silhouettes of the lions on patrol. Jumping down the rocks of the kopje, he set off across the plain to find them. It would be a lonely night, he knew, and the pride's numbers were stretched thin over the expanse of grassland. He had to check with them, if only to keep up morale, to let the sentries know they were not alone in the Bravelands night.

His paws silent on the grass, he slunk across the plain to find Noble. The young lion twisted as he approached, his muzzle peeled back from his fangs, but when he recognized his new leader he dipped his head.

"All's quiet here, Fearless. A few hyenas crossed the small river, but they didn't look threatening."

"Thanks, Noble—you're doing good work." Fearless butted

his head, then left the young lion staring out into the night, his whiskers still quivering with alertness.

Glory was next on his round, and she too looked wide awake and wary, her tail curled around her haunches, its tip twitching. She gave Fearless a nod, confirming that all was well.

"Thank you, Glory," he whispered. "Who's next in line?"

"Patient's on the other side of that small gully," murmured Glory. "In among the thornbushes. She's a clever scout. You won't see her till you're almost on top of her."

Fearless padded cautiously down the shallow rocky slope, then bounded up the other side. There was a good distance between each lion; checking each one might take all night, but it was worth it. He paused at the rim of the gully, ears pricked for any sound of Patient.

He could not hear so much as her breathing. Frowning, he pushed through scrub that caught and tugged at his fur.

"Patient?" he murmured.

He stopped. Lowering his head, he snuffed the ground. The smell of lioness was strong, and the grass was flattened and still warm. But there was no sign of Patient. Hairs rose on the nape of his neck.

"Patient," he growled again, a little more loudly.

The scent led him to a crushed patch of grass, and he narrowed his eyes. The sandy soil looked churned here, trampled in a confusion of prints, and there were dark smears and clumps of fur stuck to the thornbushes. Fearless's hide crawled as he lowered his muzzle to the black streaks on the pale earth.

Blood.

The odor was so strong, it took him a moment to catch the other scent in his flared nostrils.

Wolves!

Fearless stiffened, a low snarl rumbling from his throat. Broken twigs and scuffed pawprints led him through the darkness to a slight dip in the plain, half hidden by more scrub.

And there lay Patient in the starlight, her muzzle still curled in a terrifying snarl of fury. Her throat was torn, her tail was broken, and her ribs had been smashed open. *She died bravely.*

The wolves were gone, and Fearless knew already what he would find when he rolled her onto her back with trembling forepaws. There was a gaping void in her chest where her heart had been torn out and taken.

His horror was swiftly overtaken by a sudden terror: the wolves had broken the protective circle of lions. With a roar of fury and frustration, Fearless twisted and sprinted back the way he had come. There was no more need to be silent; he gave deep, grunting roars of summons as he ran, calling desperately to the other patrol lions.

"Noble! Glory! Bright! Sly! Back to the kopje. Harmony! *Resolute!*"

He could hear their pounding paws on the hard earth behind him, and more of his pride converging from the outer perimeter, but he couldn't spare a glance back. He bolted on, his heart pounding, until he was in sight of the kopje. It was outlined in starlight, and he could make out lanky silhouettes of wolves swarming up its ridges and outcrops.

With another roar of anger, Fearless put on a burst of speed—but almost immediately his forepaws went from under him. The ground fell away, and he almost hurtled head over heels. Catching his balance at the last moment, he staggered and skidded to a halt.

Fresh earth had been dug up and turned over. Something had been burrowing here.

As he stared, a sound drifted from within the kopje: the terrified squeal of a cub.

The others had caught him up now, and together the lions raced up the boulders and outcrops of the kopje. Fearless reached the small plateau first, just as a lion burst out of the cave mouth.

"Keen!" he bellowed in fear.

A limp wolf dangled from Keen's jaws. He flung it aside and panted for breath. "They're in the cavern, Fearless!"

Behind Keen, Valor bolted from the cave's entrance, one cub in her jaws and one stumbling and mewling in terror at her feet. Another lioness raced out behind her, a cub gripped in her jaws.

Reaching Fearless, Valor lowered her cub quickly to the ground. "The wolves dug through to the rear of the cave," she snarled. Glancing back, she saw a third lioness bound out with her cub. "But we saw them at the last moment—they didn't get any of the cubs. Honor was last out, but the wolves are behind us!"

"More fool them," growled Fearless, as a slender golden

shape streaked out of the cave, its jaws wide with slavering excitement.

Catching sight of the lions, the wolf gave a yelp of fear and tried to double back. Valor herself slammed a paw onto its back, then snatched its neck in her jaws and flung its corpse against the rocks.

Fearless bounded to the cave mouth, but no more wolves emerged. They must have retreated down their sneakily dug tunnel as soon as they realized the patrollers had returned. Fearless slammed a paw into the earth.

"We can't stay here," he snarled.

"What are we going to do?" Honor looked furious and scared, her flanks heaving. She licked her cub's head gently.

"First thing we should do is leave this place," growled Resolute.

"We can make plans as we go," said Keen, licking the blood of a wolf from his jaws. "Let's get moving."

The lions made their way in file through the darkness of the savannah night. At their head, Fearless felt all his senses buzz. Who could tell when the wolves would choose to strike again?

"Listen, Fearless." Valor trotted up to walk at his side. "These wolves will always be one step ahead. We need to turn the tables on them."

"And how would we do that?" Fearless glowered ahead into the darkness; some small creature blinked its glowing eyes in fear and fled from him.

"They're doing this for Titan, brother. Aren't they? Not for themselves." Valor gave a thoughtful grunt. "There can't be much value in the heart of a small cub—not for those brutes, anyway. Titan sent them after us out of spite and malice, and all it got for them was a couple of dead pack-mates."

"True," murmured Keen, at Fearless's rear.

"We have to convince the wolves that doing Titan's dirty work isn't worth the cost to them," said Valor grimly. "We need to be on the attack. We need to kill a lot of them, not just a few as we defend ourselves. We need to set an ambush and hunt them down."

"It's a good idea, Valor," said Fearless, "but those wolves are nothing if not smart. How are we going to trick them into an ambush?"

For a moment Valor was silent. At last Fearless paused his stride and glanced back at her, expectantly.

"With bait," she growled, gazing into his eyes. "And the cubs and I will serve as the perfect temptation."

"Valor, no!" Fearless's eyes widened. "That's far too dangerous. If something went wrong, we could lose you *and* your young ones."

"It's a danger, but not an unreasonable one. You remember what our mother used to say about hunting? *With the greatest risk comes the greatest reward.*" Valor looked fierce and determined. "I can protect my cubs, Fearless. It's up to you and the others to make a trap the wolves can't escape. Their attention will not be on my cubs for long, if you do this right."

Fearless was ready to protest further. It seemed hazardous

indeed, and yet he knew his sister so well: once Valor had decided on a course of action, there was no stopping her. Besides, what she said made sense; it was better than any plan he had devised to deal with the wolves.

"All right," he growled. "How do you plan to attract them?"

Valor bent her head to lick her cubs. "I'll take these little ones down to the river above the rapids to drink. Alone, so that the wolves expect an easy kill. But you will have an ambush waiting, and as soon as the wolves close in, you and Keen can swim across the river with the cubs. I'll stay and help the others kill the wolves." Her muzzle twisted with loathing.

"Those wolves can swim," pointed out Keen, with a glance at Fearless. "They can swim very well."

"The river is fast above the rapids," said Valor with a shrug. "I don't care whose spirits they've eaten, the wolves are scrawny creatures, built for sneaking and trickery. They can't cope with that current—but you can, and you can help the cubs. The wolves can be swept downriver, or they can stay on the shore to be killed. Their choice."

"I think it'll work," growled Resolute.

I hope you're right, thought Fearless darkly. If Valor were to lose her cubs as well as Mighty, he had a dreadful feeling it might break her.

But he could not say that aloud. "All right. We'll do it. There's no escaping the golden wolves, so we'll confront them. Let's show them what lions are made of."

* * *

Waiting in the trees above the rapids, Fearless watched Valor nudge the cubs gently toward the riverbank. She was right; the water was deep and fast here; its surface looked smooth and unthreatening, but the starlight illuminated a small broken branch that hurtled along in the current. Fearless followed its swift path until it vanished into the rapids, a few gazelle-chases downriver. The sound of the churning water reached his ears—a muted roar. Once in the rapids, skinny creatures of the wolves' size would be smashed against the rocks or dragged underwater to drown. But there was enough distance between here and the rapids to give two strong grown lions a good chance of getting the cubs to the other side. They might drift some way downstream with the flow, but he and Keen would be able to reach the far bank long before they were swept into the more dangerous, rock-filled water.

He had to have courage, Fearless told himself—at least as much courage as his sister, who padded nonchalantly toward the crumbling bank. On a sloping crescent of gritty earth, Valor crouched by the water and dipped her head to lap at it, her ears barely twitching. As she gently encouraged the cubs to join her and drink, she looked like a calm, attentive mother without a care in the world.

Fearless did not feel nearly so relaxed. He glanced at the other lions who waited with him and Keen, upwind of Valor and her cubs. He was glad to see how determined his new pride looked, how alert and tense but still.

"Be ready," he growled. "I think I smell wolf."

Keen flicked an ear back and bared his fangs silently.

Scrawny shadows were indeed moving between the trees, converging on that crescent of earth by the water's edge.

Fearless looked back at the Valorcubs. They seemed to be enjoying the adventure of a nighttime drink. The bolder cub looked very confident as he pawed at the water, splashing and scattering droplets. The other cub had wandered a little away from his mother, to nose at long grasses and bulrushes that grew in a peaceful backwater.

Valor gave that cub a glance, but the side pool was utterly calm. She focused instead on the bold cub, tapping his head with a paw and then seizing his scruff gently to draw him back from the fast-flowing main river.

His brother was gaining in boldness too, thought Fearless, half watching him as he kept his attention on the shadowy wolves. The little lion was pouncing on some imagined prey in the rushes. Then, overwhelmed by the fun of his game, he made an enormous pounce and plunged bodily into the pool.

The water erupted. For a moment Fearless did not understand, and clearly neither did the awestruck cub. Something huge reared out of the pool, water cascading from a smooth back, massive jaws opening wide in the surprised fury of a wakened sleeper. It towered above the cub, which mewled in panic.

Hippo! Fearless's heart leaped to his throat, and he tensed to spring. *But the wolves—they can't spot that I'm here—*

How the cub was not instantly trampled by the hippo, Fearless would never know. The tiny lion vanished under the hippo's stamping feet, then somehow popped up, squealing and trembling. The cub's first instinct was to run toward his mother, who had spun around at the water's edge—but the cub reached his brother first, and the two of them huddled together on the very edge of the bank, clearly too terrified to make another move. And all the time, the shadowy wolves prowled closer and closer, their circle tightening.

Valor darted frantically from side to side, trying to reach her cubs, but the hippo was roaring and stamping, swinging its massive head this way and that, and there was no way she could get through without being crushed. The hippo lunged first at her, then at the cubs; they flinched back, almost tumbling over each other, and the hippo's jaws swept above their heads.

Then, with a soft rushing sound, the muddy bank gave way. One cub gave a single terrified squeal; both vanished with the crumbling earth into the swirling current of the river.

CHAPTER TWELVE

By the dank river, green shadows lurked. Broad-trunked trees grew thickly on the sandy soil, draped in moss and crusted in lichen. The water was still, undisturbed by a single ripple. It was an eerie place, thought Thorn, and full of dangers.

"This is a bad idea," muttered Nut, as if echoing his thoughts.

"Spider's got all kinds of friends," put in Spider, chewing his lip. "But never a crocodile-friend. Not neighborly, crocodiles are. On the whole."

"At all," Nut corrected him. "They can't be trusted, Thorn. You know that."

"Even if that were true," pointed out Thorn, "I still need them. Without the crocodiles, my plan can't work. Mud, your stones said I have to bring *all* the animals of Bravelands together if I want to defeat Titan. That has to include the crocodiles, doesn't it?"

"I suppose so." Mud nodded, but he looked unhappy.

"Besides," said Thorn, "I solved the crocodiles' problem when they were in conflict with the hippos. That counts for something, and they trust me now. I've earned their help."

"It's not the crocs who have to do the trusting," said Nut darkly.

"Crocodiles can be trusted, maybe," mused Spider. "When they're not hungry." He frowned and tilted his head. "But they're hungry all the time."

"I know what the stones told me," said Mud, biting nervously on his lip, "but Thorn, please be careful. Remember that the crocodiles ate the last true Great Parent!"

Thorn didn't reply; of course he knew that. The murder of Great Mother had horrified all of Bravelands, but it had been the rhinos who drove the old elephant into the water, at Stinger's behest. The crocs had never recognized the Great Parent's authority, and they had only been doing what crocodiles do. He, Thorn, had a different relationship with them altogether.

At least, that was what he kept telling himself. "Wait here, you three."

"If you insist," muttered Nut with a twist of his muzzle. He bounded a short way back, to a sandy ridge of higher ground, and sat down firmly. "Though it breaks my heart not to chat to a crocodile."

As Mud and Spider loped to join Nut, Thorn swallowed

hard. Then he padded down onto the riverbank and stopped at the edge of the water.

At once, the eerily calm surface shivered, and ripples formed, heading straight toward him. Two eyes rose out of the water, yellow and slitted, contemplating him with hungry curiosity; then the croc revealed its long head and jaws, rimmed with savage teeth. A second surfaced beside it, then a third. The first crocodile lurched out of the water on stubby legs, tilting its head to stare at him.

If they lunged now, he wouldn't have a chance. Thorn's mouth was dry, and his heart thundered. *What was I thinking?*

Quite suddenly, his heartbeat slowed. A sense of serenity flooded over him as he stared into the eyes of the huge crocodile. *Thank you, Great Spirit*, he thought; it had given him the courage and calmness he needed.

The huge croc opened his jaws and hissed out a bone-dry, humorless laugh. "Fool of a baboon! Why have you come here?"

"I have come here," said Thorn steadily, "to speak with Rip."

"Well, Rip is not here." The croc lashed his broad tail. "Rip is upriver, basking. I am Rend, and I am in charge here, and I feel the pangs of hunger in my belly."

Drawing what strength he could from the knowledge that the Great Spirit was within him, Thorn straightened and stared back into those vicious yellow eyes.

"You do not believe in the Great Parent or the Great Spirit. I respect your belief, Rend, or your lack of it." Thorn kept his gaze fixed firmly on those of the Sandtongue-speaker. "But the crocodiles could benefit greatly if you changed that. The Great Spirit is strong, and it makes all of Bravelands' creatures stronger when we work together. You know a new threat endangers all of us."

"Hmph," snorted Rend. "The heart-eating lion?"

"Titan, yes." Thorn drew a breath. "With your help, Rend, I can defeat this new menace."

Swinging his long head, Rend glanced from side to side at his comrades. "But many of us crocodiles admire Titan," he rasped. "Indeed, we often have cause to be grateful to him. Titan leaves us many a corpse, almost intact."

"Maybe so," Thorn said through gritted fangs, "but I know that Titan has killed crocodiles, too."

Rend gave a violent lash of his knobbly tail. "Titan consumed the heart of a small and weak crocodile. Those are the ones we don't miss."

He and Rip, thought Thorn anxiously, had had an understanding; but Rend seemed to be a different proposition altogether. Besides, he was all too aware of the other crocs, who had shifted themselves into a semicircle around him, their jaws eagerly parted. None looked as if they were listening to a word he said. Thorn's fur lifted.

There was something in one croc's jaws, and Thorn peered harder. Was it prey? One small foot and a long tail hung down between her teeth. A lizard perhaps? As Thorn watched, though, the half-eaten thing moved, a small head emerged at the edge of the crocodile's mouth, and a huge eye blinked curiously at him.

Of course. The mother croc wasn't eating her tiny baby, just carrying it. These massive, fearsome creatures did have a caring side; perhaps he should try appealing to their better natures?

Thorn pointed at the baby. "Would this little one have been born, had I not intervened in the fight between you and the hippos? They would have destroyed all your eggs."

The mother croc's eyes slid sideways, to give her neighbor a thoughtful look. But Rend was not to be placated.

"You hypocrite," he spat, *"Great Father!* You never bothered yourself with Sandtongue-speakers before. As I recall, Rip had to beg for your assistance with the hippos, and crocodiles should never beg! Yet when *you* are in need? It's only then that you come to us—when you're looking for favors."

Thorn took a breath. Rend looked genuinely angry, his yellow eyes flashing, and Thorn knew he must choose his words with caution. Besides, wasn't what Rend said true?

"Yes," he said at last, "you're right. The Great Parents have not done enough to benefit the Sandtongue-speakers. There has always been an uneasy relationship between us." Thorn decided not to mention that it wasn't surprising, given that the crocodiles had actually killed the last Great Parent. "There has always been . . . too much distrust."

"Distrust?" Rend snorted. "You simply ignored us, you Great Parents. We weren't convenient, and we aren't humble enough for you."

There's nothing humble about the buffalo or leopards I talk to all the time, thought Thorn, but again he left the words unspoken. "I want to change all that, Rend. I believe that long ago, there was a better relationship between the Great Parents and the Sandtongue-speakers. Why else would the Great Spirit have given me the ability to understand your language? We were always meant to work together. And you are unique, and special," he flattered them, "but in some ways you are like the other animals of Bravelands. You want to raise your young in peace. Don't we all share that goal?" The crocodiles stared at him in silence. The mother croc let her baby wriggle around in her mouth, and its tail flopped out from the opposite row of teeth.

"While Titan lives, your offspring are at risk, just as ours are," Thorn said, watching the eyes of the mother. "Please help me put an end to that threat."

"Grab, don't look at him like that!" Rend loped on his stubby legs to the mother croc, and she twisted her head aside to protect her baby. "He does not have your infants' interests at heart, and his words are empty. If we help, he will toss us aside and ignore us as the Great Parents always have. We crocodiles can protect our own!"

Grab eyed Rend for a moment, then dipped her head beneath the water.

Not only had his mission failed, but Thorn knew he was in real danger. The slitted yellow eyes of the crocodiles looked downright hostile now. He began to edge backward. Perhaps it was time to cut his losses and get out of here—

"Great Father Thorn?" A deep, rasping bellow interrupted the tense standoff.

Thorn felt a rush of relief as a familiar crocodile lurched from the river, shunted Rend aside, and loped up the shore. "Greetings, Rip!"

"What are you doing here?" growled the big croc. Water streamed from his thick leathery scales. "Never thought I'd lay eyes on *you* again."

"Just what I was saying," muttered Rend behind him.

"I've come to request your help," said Thorn quickly and politely. "Your assistance in dealing with Titan Wolfpride."

"*Dealing with?* Kill him, I hope you mean," rasped Rip. "That brute causes too much damage, however much carrion he leaves behind him."

"I agree," said Thorn, puffing out a sigh of relief. "So what do you say, Rip?"

The huge crocodile narrowed his eyes and lifted his enormous head to stare at the three baboons on the sandbank beyond Thorn. "Those are your friends? I'll escort you back to them."

There were rebellious grunts from the other crocs as Rip pounded heavily up the shore at Thorn's side. Nut, Mud, and Spider watched the odd pair approach, their eyes wide and nervous. Thorn was glad to see that they held their ground, though Mud swallowed hard and shuddered.

Rip halted at the foot of the low sandbank, and Thorn bounded up to join his friends. Rip glared up at all four of them; Thorn found it impossible to read his expression.

"Congratulations on not getting eaten, Thorn," said Nut dryly.

"Is that one going to eat *us*, though?" asked Spider. "He's mighty big."

"I don't think so." Thorn turned back warily to Rip. "Well, Rip? What do you say to an alliance?"

"That depends," said Rip. "Tell me your whole plan, Great Father."

Thorn took a deep breath. "The crocodiles are rulers of the Bravelands rivers," he began tactfully. "No creature can withstand you in your own territory—not even the mighty Titan. If we can lure him close enough to the water—perhaps even into it—I know that you and your bask could make short work of him. That would give you a fitting revenge, Rip—and prove to the other animals of Bravelands that you deserve their gratitude as well as their respect."

Rip's yellow eyes narrowed. "But what would lure Titan into our waters? Hmm?"

"I have a feeling he'll go voluntarily," said Thorn. "In fact it's not just a feeling; I'm sure that's what he plans. The Great Parent has always entered the water to accept the leadership of Bravelands. How could a tyrant like Titan resist that symbolic act? We just have to make sure you and your comrades are waiting for him. I don't care how many spirits he has consumed; he cannot stand against your kind."

Rip nodded thoughtfully. The other three baboons had retreated farther back on the sandbank, but they watched Thorn and Rip's conversation with wide, uncomprehending eyes. The other crocodiles watched too, their eyes and heads just visible, and the jagged ridges of their tails. Their attention was riveted on Thorn and their leader.

"Titan can certainly take down one crocodile, or even two," rasped Rip. "You know, one of the crocs he killed was my own son, Tear."

"I'm sorry," murmured Thorn, dipping his head.

"I have many sons and daughters," growled Rip, "but Tear was the strongest and finest."

"That fits with Titan's ways," observed Thorn. "He takes the most powerful spirits and targets leaders."

"If he could take down Tear, no crocodile is safe." Rip's eyes narrowed. "But you are right, Baboon: even Titan cannot stand against a whole bask of us. I will carry your proposal to them, and to other crocodiles farther upstream, beyond the Muddy River Rapids. It is possible for us to take down Titan, but I need agreement from all my comrades. I will state your case as well as I can, believe me." His jaws parted wider to show his savage teeth. "I want vengeance for Tear."

The huge crocodile turned, with a sweep of his enormous tail, and slid silently back into the water. When he and his bask had submerged, leaving barely a ripple, Mud, Nut, and Spider padded cautiously down the sandbank toward Thorn.

"What did he say?" asked Mud, as Spider peered curiously at the river.

"He's on our side, at least," said Thorn. "Rip wants to help; he just has to convince his bask. But I think he can do it—he's a charismatic and powerful leader, Mud. I have hope for this plan!"

"I still don't like working with crocs," said Mud with a

shiver, "but if you trust them, Thorn, then I do too."

"What's that commotion?" asked Spider suddenly. He tilted his head and frowned upriver.

"Lions?" said Nut doubtfully. "I think I hear lions. . . ."

"Yes." Thorn bounded to the edge of the bank and peered hard. "I hear roaring. What's going on?"

"It's not Titan, is it?" asked Mud anxiously.

"No, it isn't." Thorn sucked in a breath. Surely he must be mistaken, but . . . that sounded like Fearless's voice . . . ? Yes, he was sure of it. And though Thorn could not make out the words, his friend sounded terrified.

Thorn did not hesitate. Rising up on his hind paws, he closed his eyes and reached out with his mind, scanning the riverbanks, searching for the familiar lion. He pinpointed Fearless quickly and dived into his head without a second thought.

Thorn blinked. He felt strange: powerful and muscular and huge. Until this moment, he hadn't truly realized just how much Fearless had grown: he was in the body of a fully grown lion.

But there was helpless terror in his heart.

He bolted downstream, his mane blowing back with his speed. He bounded over tree roots and fallen branches, hardly caring where he put his paws. All the while, he scanned the river's surface, desperate and afraid. And suddenly he could see something in middle of the river—no, two somethings, unreachable, bobbing helplessly in the fast current. Small heads—

Lion cubs! And however fast he ran, he could not keep up with the current of the stream. The cubs drew farther and farther away. They had survived the tumble through the rapids—perhaps because they were so small and sturdy and resilient—but they would not survive the wolves: the golden wolves, whose shapes flickered through the trees and scrub far ahead, lithe and quick and deadly.

Two of the wolves emerged from the riverbank scrub and flung themselves into the water, jaws eagerly parted. But they were caught in the midstream current and swept past the cubs, whining and yelping. Other wolves stayed on dry land, racing ahead.

They must not reach the Valorcubs!

Thorn's heart thrashed with terror as he made the leap from Fearless's head to the closest cub. He plunged into the little lion's mind, and it was worse than the cold grip of the river: such uncomprehending terror and panic. He was bruised and battered from the rapids, and *all he wanted was his mother. Mother! Mother, help me!*

There was nothing Thorn could do here to help. He cast around frantically with his mind and found one of the wolves, the one who led the pack. He made the leap and found himself immersed in hungry bloodthirst, and a rising, heart-pounding excitement. *We will have them, we will have them! Soon!*

CHAPTER THIRTEEN

There was nothing Fearless could do. He felt like a helpless cub again himself as he watched the two little lions swirl in the current. He willed them to catch hold of something—anything—that would save them, but whenever a branch swirled by or they were swept past a jutting boulder, they would snatch for it, only to lose their grip straightaway. They simply did not have the strength in their small paws to save themselves.

My sister can't lose her cubs, too. She can't!

"More wolves!" Keen's roar of warning came from behind him, but Fearless didn't glance back. He saw immediately where the danger lay. Three wolves had padded out onto the trunk of a fallen tree, downstream, and they waited there, shoulders hunched in expectation. They grinned, licking their drooling jaws. The rushing water crashed into the tree, mounting up in a constant foaming wave, as the cubs were swept closer.

Fearless's heart lurched. It would be the work of a moment for the waiting wolves to snatch the cubs from the water. He pounded faster, his paws raising clouds of dust.

And then, miraculously, one of the little lions snatched at a tangle of sodden branches in the stream and kept his grip. His foreleg stretched and stretched, but his claws dug desperately into the mass of floating wood. He hauled himself, dripping and shaking, onto the raft of branches.

The brave cub hadn't abandoned his sibling, though. As the second cub drifted close, mewling in terror, he managed to lunge down and grab one paw with his tiny teeth and claws. There was turmoil for a moment, as the cub who was still in the water flailed and splashed and squealed. But with a massive tug, his brother pulled him onto the branches beside him.

The ramshackle island was buffeted by the current, but it didn't float downstream. Fearless realized it must be caught on a root or a rock underwater. But how long could it stay there in this torrent? The two cubs were only a couple of leaps away from the slavering wolves on the log—and both little ones looked very unsteady on their paws.

"Hold on!" Fearless roared. "Keep as still as you can!"

A great yipping and howling rose from the excited wolves on the dead tree. One of them slammed both his forepaws in frustration against the wet bark; his neighbor, unable to contain herself, made a sudden leap toward the island of branches.

She fell well short. In less than a moment, the current had caught her and she was whirled downstream, vanishing under the surface with a snuffed-out yelp.

But her companions were not dissuaded. A second, male wolf tried to make the jump to the cubs. This one hooked his front claws into the tangled twigs. The river yanked at him, but he held on, grinning, his tongue lolling as foam splashed up into his face.

The wolf wasn't letting go, Fearless realized, and at any moment he could pull himself up onto the island and take the cubs. Fearless could bear it no longer. He sprang with all his might, plunging into the river in a shower of white spray.

The current was even worse than he had expected. It snatched at him, trying to drag him away from the cubs. Flailing his legs as hard as he could, gritting his fangs, and closing his nostrils against the spray, Fearless struggled toward the cubs and their sanctuary island.

The wolf was still hanging on by its claws, and bit by bit it was heaving itself up onto the island. Fearless gasped, then coughed, as water filled his mouth. He tried to shake himself and forged on, battling the strength of the current.

Through half-blinded eyes, he saw the third wolf make its leap from the log: this cunning brute had thought it through. It sprang for the wolf that clutched the edge of the branches, landed square on his back, and used him as a launching point to leap to the island. The wolf in the water lost his grip and hurtled downriver, howling.

But the one who had used him as a stepping-stone was

safely on the island of branches. He stalked forward, grinning at the two cowering Valorcubs.

It's over. A tide of despair swamped Fearless, and his legs faltered. He was so close, but still too far away. He watched the wolf pad delicately forward, flaring its nostrils, enjoying the moment. "Ah, little ones. I take your hearts for our master, Titan!"

One cub shrank back, quivering, but the other stood foursquare, opening its jaws to give a squeaky roar of defiance. The wolf smacked him idly with a paw, rolled him onto his back, and watched him squirm.

The less-bold cub could clearly take it no more. He bounded forward to defend his brother, but the wolf simply swiped him onto his flank and pinned him with his other paw. The wolf looked from cub to cub, licking his lips.

Fearless didn't want to watch. But he had to. *For Valor, I have to. I tried, Valor!*

A shadow, vast and broad, darkened the sky above the wolf, which turned for a moment from its prey. Fearless saw it was an eagle. Its square wingtips flared, and it dived toward the wolf, raking its huge talons into the pale golden flank.

Shocked, the wolf howled and dodged. But the island was not a good place to try a fast maneuver. He stumbled and toppled sideways into the river. It swallowed him instantly.

Fearless's heartbeat hammered in his throat. Would the cubs escape the wolf, only to be taken by an eagle? Despair gripped him as two more eagles swooped down toward the island, each one seizing a cub's scruff in its talons, before carrying aloft. Another wave of water foamed over Fearless's face, making him splutter and falter. Heart heavy with grief, Fearless let the current twist him around, carrying him backward downstream. His eyes searched the sky for the eagles, but to his astonishment he saw they weren't carrying the cubs away. Instead, they flew right toward the shore, where a panting Valor stood there, her flanks heaving, her face riven with terror and shock.

The eagles spread their wings and landed, depositing the cubs gently in front of her.

Fearless sucked in a breath and began to kick and paddle again. He did not understand, but Valor had fallen on her cubs, licking and licking them till they tumbled over. The eagles flapped into nearby trees and perched there, gazing down dispassionately. With a surge of energy, Fearless fought the current, battling to steer himself back to shore.

His claws raked against thick river mud, and he scrabbled for better purchase. There was a tumble of boulders against the bank, and he dragged himself up them and out of the water. Shaking his fur violently, water scattering from his mane, he stood for a moment, catching his breath, calming his heart. Then he sprinted back up the shore to where Valor stood over her cubs.

Keen loped to his side. "There are still wolves around," he panted. "But look. The eagles are helping us!"

As he and Keen stared, Fearless was aware of the rest of his pride running to join them, but he couldn't spare them a glance. He was riveted by the spectacle of the eagles, who harried and drove the remaining wolves, clawing at them with their talons, screeching violently.

A few tried to snap and fight back, but it was hopeless. One by one, they fell back, tumbling over the edge and into the river. Fearless watched, speechless with astonishment, as the last golden wolf gave a yelp, staggered, and was swallowed up in the rushing water.

At once, the noise of screeching and whistling and hooting was silenced. The birds rose up into the higher air.

"What the—" said Resolute, but he fell silent, his jaws hanging open.

"I never saw anything like that," whispered Noble in awe.

"What just happened?" Glory swung her head, gazing at her pride-mates. "The birds saved the cubs! They came from nowhere. . . ."

"I can explain!" called a voice from the far bank.

Fearless spun around with a surge of joy. Thorn stood on the far bank, grinning with delight. The baboon eyed the river, bit his lip, then began to leap. Light and sure-footed, he found submerged rocks and tussocks, pausing only for an instant on each before making his next jump. He reached the floating island of branches, then sprang onto the tree where the wolves had waited and bounded to join the lions.

Fearless loped to meet him, dipping his head to receive a hug from his old friend. But before he could speak, Valor had padded to their side.

"You did this?" she asked the baboon. *"You!"*

Thorn nodded, a little shyly. "It's the birds. They understand me. And they're helpful sorts—"

"But this is *amazing*," said Keen, staring at Thorn in disbelief.

Fearless licked Keen's face. "So do you believe in the Great Father now, old friend?"

"Do I!" exclaimed Keen.

"And the rest of you?" said Fearless.

Behind Keen the remainder of the pride growled with uncertainty, as if they still couldn't quite comprehend what they had seen, or what they were hearing.

But Valor stepped in front of Thorn and dipped her head low. "Thank you, Great Father. *Thank you.*"

For a moment Thorn looked embarrassed, scratching at his muzzle and glancing from side to side. "It was my pleasure, Valor. Really it was. You're Fearless's sister."

"All the same, you did not have to help." She raised her head and gazed solemnly into his eyes. "I will never forget this kindness, Great Father Thorn."

Some of the other lions dropped their heads too, though half a dozen remained haughty and erect. Clearly, the idea of being submissive in front of a baboon was too much for them.

"Pride-mates!" roared Fearless. "Follow the lead of my sister and Keen! There is no shame in giving thanks to the Great Spirit."

"But . . ." began Noble, licking his muzzle nervously.

"Did you not witness Thorn's powers?" snapped Valor. "Did you not see him bend the birds to his will?"

"Actually," muttered Thorn, "I just asked them nicely if they wouldn't mind . . ."

"Not helpful," said Fearless, under his breath. "Lions respect strength."

"Oh, right," said Thorn. "How about this?"

With that, he jumped up, landing neatly on Fearless's back. Raising both arms above his head, he hooted loudly. "Come, my flocks! Show these unbelievers the power of the Great Spirit! Let them see the power of Bravelands!"

For a moment, nothing happened. The assembled lions fidgeted, scraping at the ground with their paws. But then the eagles returned.

Not just eagles... Fearless realized.

The sky was filled suddenly with birds: egrets, hawks, blue starlings, bee-eaters and weaver birds, a hornbill, and a marabou stork. Lions snarled and roared with unease as the birds flew in a great cloud as if they shared a single mind. Thorn lowered his arms with a sudden thrashing gesture, and the swarm wheeled and dived in unison, swooping low enough over the heads of the pride that some ducked away in fear. After a single pass, they separated again into their own flocks and flew away.

"Does anyone doubt now?" asked Fearless of his startled pride.

"We hail the Great Father," roared Resolute suddenly.

"All hail!" added Noble.

"Yes!" The other lions joined in, scraping their claws into the ground, throwing back their heads. "The Great Father Baboon!"

Thorn hopped down beside Fearless. His lips were

stretched wide with a smile of pride.

"It wasn't too much?" whispered the baboon as the lions roared their approval.

"Just right," replied Fearless.

As the cheers died, Valor began to fuss over her cubs, licking the moisture from their sodden fur. The bolder cub shook his head, making a face, as her tongue lashed between his ears yet again, but he submitted. The other cub butted close against his mother's leg, begging for his share of his mother's attention, and she turned once more to him. Both Valorcubs were bruised and scratched from their wild ride through the rapids, but otherwise they seemed unharmed.

When the two little ones were thoroughly dry—or rather, wet and spike-furred from her licking instead—Valor lifted her head. She nodded at Thorn and at Fearless, and then turned to the pride.

"I am ready to name my cubs," she declared.

The Valorcubs gasped in excitement, clambering over each other as they tried to reach her legs. "Momma! Really? Names?"

"Yes, names." She laughed softly, nuzzling their heads. "You've earned them already, Valorcubs." She gave a coughing grunt to clear her throat and raised her voice to speak clearly.

"This older cub, who stood up so bravely to the wolf on the island: I name him *Gallant.*"

"Gallant!" echoed the cub, gamboling in delight.

"His brother, who came to his side when the wolf took him: I name him *Loyal.*"

As the lions of the pride roared their approval, Fearless remained silent. His heart was too full to say anything. Valor had honored not only their shared father, but she had also paid tribute to Loyal, Fearless's blood parent.

"Thank you, Valor," he muttered. "You've chosen well. The names are perfect."

She licked his ear. "I wanted to thank our fathers for giving us life and teaching us to survive Bravelands. But how can we repay Thorn the baboon?" She lifted her head to gaze into his eyes. "Great Father, I don't think it's possible. I'll never be able to thank you enough for the lives of my cubs."

"Well, there is something." Thorn fidgeted on Fearless's back and cleared his throat.

"Just say it, and it's yours," urged Keen.

"Will you come to the Great Gathering tomorrow? Will Fearlesspride represent the lions of Bravelands?"

It was astonishing that he was able to ask it, thought Fearless, and it was a brave request. But the lions did not even hesitate. They chorused their grunting agreement.

"We will be there."

"Fearlesspride will be at the Great Gathering."

"For you, Thorn. For what you did today."

Thorn trembled, his paws clutching tightly on Fearless's mane. "This means more than you can imagine," he said hoarsely. His voice rose. "If the lions are with me, I have a better chance than ever of defeating Titan. I already have the crocodiles as allies, and with Fearlesspride too, our hopes are high. Let me tell you my plan. . . ."

The crocodiles. Fearless couldn't help the stiffening of his muscles, the lifting of his hackles. Thorn was clever and brave, but as he listened to his old friend outline his plan to the lions, Fearless felt a deep foreboding. Titan wasn't just a hard lion to beat—as a cunning trickster himself, he was just as hard to fool.

It didn't matter, thought Fearless. *If anything goes wrong with Thorn's plan, I'll be there. And this time, I won't fail. I'll put an end to Titan at long last.*

CHAPTER FOURTEEN

The blue-grayness of the dawn savannah became a pale misty gold; beyond the mountains to the east, the violet sky was streaked with amber. Light began to find the forests, turning them from vague lilac outlines to a sprawl of gilded green. The gray plain turned to yellow and ocher as sunbeams spilled over the horizon, and the watering hole, burnished silver, reflected the high streaks of cloud in the sky.

Sky stood in the long shadow of a gangly acacia, her heart thumping with nerves. The elephant herds milled a short distance away, their ears flapping with nervous anticipation. Only the calves, and Nimble and Lively at her feet, seemed to be simply enjoying the sunrise.

Sky had no idea whether the animals of Bravelands would respond to her summons. Titan had struck so much fear into so many hearts, she would not even blame the herds if they chose to stay away; to follow the example of the Great Father who they thought had fled in fear. How had the Great Spirit protected them lately? Even the firmest faith must waver in times like these. But if no creatures came to the Great Gathering, then Thorn's plan would all be for nothing.

Oh, Great Spirit. Let them come.

Titan had to come too, of course, if Thorn's scheme was to succeed. Sky was not nearly so eager for that lion to turn up, but of course he must. This might be their last opportunity to defeat him for a very long time—or at all.

"Sky," said Rock. He reached out his trunk to curl it around hers. "We have done all we can. *You* have done more than could ever have been expected. If the Great Spirit is with us, and watching, I know all will be well."

"I hope the Spirit is near," she whispered. "Rock, this could all go so wrong. We could see our friends die today. We ourselves might not survive."

"Courage, Sky. Our friends are watching. We have to look certain for their sakes."

Rock was right. Though they tried not to stare, Sky was aware that the gazes of the gathered elephants kept turning toward her. She swallowed hard, wishing that the Great Father were here.

She scanned the landscape. Thorn would not show himself until he needed to, but even if he was not physically close by, Sky knew he would be watching everything through the eyes of another creature. Perhaps a vulture? The great birds were swooping out of the sky right now, alighting in the branches of the surrounding trees, stretching their wings, hunching their shoulders to wait. Recognizing Windrider, Sky gave the old bird a respectful nod.

There was movement out on the savannah; Sky gave a small gasp of excitement. Creatures were coming . . . a pair of shy dik-diks picked their way nervously toward the watering hole. They glanced warily at a pod of hippos that thundered up from the riverbank, churning it to mud. A vast mass of black buffalo raised a cloud of sun-gilded dust as they moved across the plain toward the elephants. Zebras and wildebeests approached from another direction, and a troop of vervets bounded from the direction of the distant forest, chattering and screeching.

Soon there were too many to count the different herds, and Sky's heart soared. Silhouetted against the rising sun, more and more animals trekked across the grassland: hyenas, impalas, three elegant giraffes. Another zebra herd approached, accompanied by gazelles and a pair of bushbuck. Even the earth came alive with small creatures: ground squirrels, rats and hares and hyraxes. A serval cat stalked toward them, alone and aloof, averting its gaze very determinedly from a family of mice; hunting was forbidden during a Great Gathering.

Sky realized she need not have worried. The herds kept coming, and before long she was wondering if this might be the largest Great Gathering she had ever witnessed. A leopard bounded through the grass. A coalition of cheetahs approached from the opposite direction, lithe and sleek. A pack of wild dogs trotted between the grass-eaters, huge ears pricked high.

One of the wild dogs skittered indignantly aside as three baboons bounded straight through the pack. Mud, Nut, and Spider loped toward Sky, their eyes bright with excitement.

"Sky." Nut stopped in front of her trunk and nodded. "We're the only baboons so far, I'm afraid. I've kept an eye out for Dawntrees Troop as we traveled here, but there's no sign they've left Brightforest." He sighed.

"Don't worry," Sky reassured him. "Look how many have come to the Gathering! This is going to work, Nut."

"Wait." Mud loped a few paces to the side and craned to see over the herds. "I can't be seeing what I'm seeing. . . ."

"What?" Spider's eyes opened wide with curiosity. He grabbed hold of Nut and scrambled onto his shoulders, ignoring Nut's yells of indignation. Nut swayed and cursed, but Spider hung on to his head and stood up on Nut's shoulder blades, balancing carefully. "Wow. Mud, you're right! Lions!"

"Lions?" Rock's ears flapped forward, and he frowned. "Titan, already?"

"No, that's not Titan," said Mud. "I'd recognize that brute anywhere, and there aren't any wolves."

"Surely they aren't here to hunt," exclaimed Sky in horror. "Even lions wouldn't intentionally disrespect a Great Gathering."

"No." A broad smile spread over Mud's features. "That's Fearless and his pride!"

"Fearless? His pride too?" cried Sky.

The other animals seemed to be just as shocked. One by one, the herds and predators turned to stare as the lion pride stalked toward the water's edge.

"I want to see," protested Nut. He shook Spider off, put a paw on his head, and clambered up, swapping places.

"Lions do not follow the Great Parent," muttered Rock to Sky. "What are they up to? Fearless I could understand, but his whole pride?"

"That's his sister, Valor," said Mud, as the lions drew closer.

"And his pride's gotten much bigger," observed Nut. "Where's that other lion? Whatshisname, Mighty?"

"I don't know." Sky waited in trepidation as Fearless detached himself from the pride and paced forward alone. "Fearless. Welcome."

Fearless bowed his head respectfully. His mane really had grown quickly, thought Sky distractedly, and it was going to be impressive.

"Thank you, Sky Strider," said Fearless formally. He lowered his voice. "My pride has come at Thorn's request, and they have respect for the Gathering and its traditions."

Sky blew out a quiet breath of relief. "Where is Thorn?" she murmured.

"He's watching from the forest," Fearless told her, adding wryly, "and probably from a few of these grass-eaters' heads. He'd get a good vantage point from that giraffe."

Sky couldn't help but smile. "I feel better knowing he's here somewhere."

"And he'll put in an appearance when the time is right," Fearless assured her quietly.

Sky cleared her throat and took a decisive step forward. Around the watering hole, the hosts of animals stilled their hooves and voices.

"Thank you all. For attending this Great Gathering, I am grateful to you; after all, we had no Great Parent to summon you." She lowered her eyes, guilty at the lie. She could only hope the herds would mistake the tremor in her voice for grief. "This has been a terrible season, after many dreadful ones. I can confirm to you all that we have lost our beloved Great Father, Thorn the baboon."

"We'd heard that already," snapped a hyena. "He scarpered like a scared mouse? So what are we here for?"

A group of wildebeests stirred restlessly, and their leader pawed the earth with a hoof. "This whole Gathering is irregular, Sky Strider," he said with a glare at the lions. "Are we going to get a new Great Parent?"

"I hope we haven't come all this way for nothing," called a giraffe from the rear.

A few rodents squeaked in haughty agreement at Sky's feet. A leopard gave an impatient growl and glared at the elephants.

Sky glanced anxiously around. She couldn't blame them for their frustration. This Great Gathering had provoked much gossip and excitement on the plains and in the forests; no wonder the animals were impatient to know what it was all about.

"I hope it's not another baboon," bellowed a buffalo, and

his herd grunted in agreement.

"That's not fair—" began Sky, but a gerenuk interrupted her.

"We need a good strong leader," she brayed. "One that can take on Titan and defeat him!"

"I knew from the start that baboon was wrong for the job," grumbled a hippo.

"He's probably sunning himself on a branch in a distant forest, fat on juicy fruit," agreed the surly leopard. "Everyone knows baboons are idle at heart."

Sky longed to trumpet in anger at them all. *If only you knew what Thorn had done, and is still doing, for all of you!* But she swallowed the words and stood in silence. It was so important to let them all go on thinking Thorn was dead.

Where are you, Titan? I know you must be here. Show yourself!

Just as she thought it, there was a squeal of terror from a sounder of warthogs at the edge of the Gathering. They bolted into a run, almost crashing into a herd of gazelles. The gazelles, turning to complain, went stock-still, then skittered away themselves, pronking and dodging.

The murmurs of dissatisfaction from the whole horde turned to squeals and bellows of panic, as Titan prowled through the broad gap that opened to make way for him. Zebras flinched away, whinnying in fear; a giraffe lurched into a run. Behind Titan stalked his wolf pack, fangs glittering, jaws hanging wide in gleeful grins.

Sky stared at the massive lion, and suddenly she felt her faith in Thorn's plan waver. Surely Titan, already a full-grown lion, had become unnaturally huge? His presence seemed to darken the dawn, his shadow spilling before him like darkness with a mind of its own. His smooth movements crackled with power, and his yellow fangs gleamed as he snarled at the animals he passed. The herds pressed back so desperately, Sky was afraid that some smaller creatures might be crushed. Truly, she believed that Titan could kill with the power of fear alone.

Beside her, Fearless was silent, but his hide and mane bristled. Sky could sense the hatred emanating from him. His muzzle peeled back from his fangs, but he didn't move.

Titan came to a halt, right beneath the tree in which the vultures perched. They stared down at him, unmoving.

He turned to face the gathered herds, surveying them with an air of absolute dominance.

"Creatures of Bravelands. Poor, weak creatures, living your lives in fear. I, Titan Wolfpride, bring you great news."

Not a hoof scraped, not a growl escaped a predator's throat. Even the mice crouched quietly in the grass. Every scared eye was fixed on Titan.

Titan's voice boomed like thunder. "You all know me, and you know my strength. Your Great Father has abandoned you. He sent another—his own mate—to die at my jaws so that he himself could flee. I have sensed him spying on me and tasted his fear. But he is gone now, never to return. If this Great Spirit occupied his heart, it too has run away."

A little jackal whimpered and was shushed by its mother; there was no other sound.

"Power over Bravelands is mine," Titan went on, his glossy black mane rippling as he flexed his huge shoulder muscles. "Lions have always been your natural leaders, and I, as the leader of lions, come to claim my right of rule. My first edict: forget your petty Code. I revoke it from this moment, and in its place my single rule applies: the strongest will survive. I, Titan, am the strongest of all, and you will bow before me. Follow me to the water, every one of you. Do you see how I respect your traditions and customs?" Titan turned with a flick of his tail and prowled the few paces down to the riverbank. "Drink with me and show me your respect." A sly light came into his eye as he glanced back at the herds. "Obey or die, here and now."

With a single, soaring bound, Titan plunged into the water. He rose up in a fountain of spray and stood tall, up to his belly, water streaming from his mane and shoulders, his coat gleaming darkly in the sunlight.

"Respect!" he roared. "Now!"

Sky could bear it no longer. She thundered forward to face him, glaring straight into his black glittering eyes. Then she turned back to the gathered herds and raised her trunk.

"Stand firm, all of you!" she cried. "This creature cannot cow the Great Spirit!"

The animals looked from Titan to Sky, and back again. It was as if, in that moment, they didn't know who scared them more. The wolves were slinking forward, growling as they formed a semicircle around Sky, but she ignored them. Fearless was watching her intently, his tail lashing. He looked coiled to spring at Titan. *No, Fearless,* she willed him. *Don't make your move, not now.*

"You." Sky turned furiously on Titan once more. "You are nothing but a Codebreaking murderer, and you have no place in Bravelands."

"Says you, a mad elephant who cannot even walk with her herd!" Titan slammed a massive paw into the water in a shower of glittering spray. With deliberate contempt, he averted his gaze from her and glared once more at the herds. "Perhaps one of you wish to challenge me? Come, seize your moment of glory! Be remembered for this day! Let your heart be ripped out and consumed; why not? Let your weak spirit live in me and feel true power for the first time!"

Sky's mouth was as dry as old bones on the Plain of Our Ancestors. *Oh, Thorn,* she found herself pleading inwardly. *Thorn. Now is the time, or never!*

CHAPTER FIFTEEN

Fearless prowled to Sky's side. His paws trembled with the longing to rip out Titan's throat, to silence that boastful, booming roar forever. Sky had barely had time to outline Thorn's plan as they waited, and her rapid explanation had not calmed his fears. He had been here before, he thought bitterly. *Then, I had to stand back to let Mighty fight; now, still, I must wait!* Fearless wanted to trust Thorn completely; he respected his cleverness. But could this outcome really be any different?

As his muscles tensed with frustration and loathing, he felt Sky's trunk touch his shoulder gently.

"No, Fearless," she whispered urgently. "We have to follow through with Thorn's plan."

Titan's triumphant sneer was almost unbearable to see. The morning sun outlined his black mane in a haze of gold;

he looked, thought Fearless with a lurch in his gut, like a vision of supreme victory.

The herds were creeping forward now, one animal at a time, approaching the bank. They were afraid, Fearless knew. Some would make the decision to survive, to enter the water to drink with Titan. Then others would follow, faster and faster, and eventually all the creatures of Bravelands would submit to this tyrant. Anger surged hot in Fearless's throat.

Then something stirred in the river beyond Titan, ripples that became sharp-pointed waves. Fearless laid back his ears, holding his breath.

"Titan's day has come," Sky whispered to him.

Ridged backs rose from the water as the crocodiles surfaced. Titan was hemmed in by a semicircle of them, their slitted eyes fixed on him. His gaze passed over them, but he barely moved.

At once, the herds erupted in screams and howls and hoots of alarm. A zebra gave a braying cry of terror.

"Crocodiles!"

"They're coming for us all!" squealed a warthog.

"No!" trumpeted Sky. "Calm yourselves!"

One by one, the animals around her turned to stare. They looked from Sky to the circling crocodiles, their ears flicking, hooves stamping. One or two exchanged mutters and nervous cries, but Sky's order had stilled them. Trembling, the herds turned to stare at Titan, and at the ridged heads and backs that now homed in on him.

Fearless dared to believe that Thorn's plan was going to work.

Murmurs of disbelief and a growing excitement went through all the creatures. The wildebeests grunted and pawed the ground. The leopard sat up on its haunches, its grumpy expression changing to one of eager fascination. Farther back, a gazelle pronked, eager to see past its herd-mates. A great chirruping and squeaking arose from the smaller creatures. The animals that had moved toward Titan now drew back, their heads lifting, their expressions of defeated terror replaced now with relief. As the crocodiles closed in on Titan, the noise became a swelling chorus of roars, hoots, whistles, and cheers.

Fearless remained silent, his claws digging hard into the shoreline mud, as he stared at Titan. He should be glad, but all he felt was a bone-deep frustration. This should have been his moment. He should have been the one to kill Titan, yet Sky and Thorn had stolen his moment of glory and given it to a bask of vicious Sandtongue-hissers.

"Look, Fearless!" said Sky. "That's Rip, the leader of the Muddy River Bask. Titan killed his son. I know this must be hard for you, but others have lost family to that mad lion. The crocodiles have the best chance of all of us. And Rip is owed this!"

"I'm owed it too," growled Fearless, "and Titan doesn't look afraid."

"That's only because he's mad," said Sky grimly. "Don't

worry, Fearless. He's doomed. There's no way he can escape."

Titan looked from side to side. He eyed the crocodiles, his face impassive. Then he turned back toward the animals on the bank.

Throwing his head back, he gave a roar. "So this is your plan to defeat me?" There wasn't so much as a quaver in his voice. "You dare not face me yourselves, so you have these crocodiles do your dirty work?"

Something's wrong, thought Fearless. *Why isn't he trying to escape?*

After a brief moment, Rip lunged toward Titan, jaws agape. As he closed in on the mad lion, the other crocs surged too. But not toward Titan. Savage jaws clamped around Rip's tail, dragging him back.

Rip had no time for anger; he looked astonished as he was pulled under by the other crocodile. Fearless snapped his head around to stare at Sky. *This was part of the plan?*

But Sky looked almost as confused as Rip. Her eyes widened, and her mouth opened a little. Rock gave a trumpet of horror.

Rip surfaced again, struggling and flailing, as the other crocodiles broke their circle around Titan and turned on their leader. Rip's jaws opened in a bellow of shock and fury as he vanished in a turmoil of lashing tails and spinning bodies and foaming river water.

"What?" Fearless gave a roar of despair as the crocs snapped and tore, and a dark cloud of blood stained the water. "Sky! What is this?"

"I don't—I don't know—" Sky took a step backward, shaking her ears. "No, *no*—"

Something floated to the surface as the crocodiles withdrew, something pale and scaly. Rip drifted there, lifeless, his belly exposed, torn to pieces by his own bask.

Calmly, without any urgency at all, Titan turned in the water. He seized Rip's foreleg in his jaws and dragged him backward out of the river.

The herds stampeded and wheeled, but Fearless could only gape in silence, his flanks heaving. He could hardly bear to look as Titan set about Rip's corpse, tearing at the dead crocodile's tough hide. Titan plunged his head into the cavity of his chest, and Fearless lowered his eyes. It was obvious the morsel he was searching for. When Fearless looked again, Titan's face and muzzle were drenched in blood. He held Rip's heart in his jaws.

"No," Sky was still crying. "This isn't possible."

The crocodiles of Rip's bask drifted in the water, as they watched Titan devour the heart and spirit of their former leader.

"He outwitted you again," snarled Fearless to Sky. "You and Thorn both. He found out about your plan and approached the crocodiles himself. He convinced them to betray their leader. To betray you. To betray *all of us.*"

"But," cried Sky, bewildered, "*how?* How could he even communicate with crocs? He can't speak Sandtongue!"

"Maybe he can," spat Fearless. "How many spirits of

Sandtongue-speakers has he devoured? Snakes, lizards—according to you, he ate the heart of Rip's own son!"

Sky fell silent, her eyes tormented. Mud, Nut, and Spider ran to her side, and Keen trotted behind them.

"There's more to this," growled Keen, padding to Fearless's side. "Think for a moment. If Titan knew about Thorn's plan all along, that means he knows Thorn hasn't run away."

Fearless's eyes widened. "Thorn could be in terrible danger."

Rock pressed his shoulder against Sky's, and Mud touched her leg gently. Nut stared at the carnage by the river. All the while, the crocodiles sniggered. Panic had gripped the gathered herds; they stampeded wildly, crushing smaller animals beneath their hooves, colliding with one another, snapping and biting in their desperation to escape.

"That was the strongest croc in Bravelands!" neighed a zebra, high-pitched and terrified.

"Titan has the crocodiles on his side now!" squealed an impala.

"We're doomed!" bellowed a buffalo. "Get our calves away from here! Get away!"

Wildebeests, warthogs, giraffes and gerenuks, hippos and hyraxes: they all shoved and struck out, struggling to flee up the sandbank and away from the bloodstained water, where Titan postured triumphantly over the corpse of Rip.

Fearless and his friends could only stare at the scene in anger and desperation. Nut picked up a stone and flung it in frustration after a fleeing buffalo.

"That's no good *at all*," pointed out Spider, shrugging.

"Spider's right," said Mud. "We need to calm down. Think. This is an emergency!"

Sky looked too horrified even to speak; Rock was murmuring gently to her. Keen glared at Titan and his crocodile allies. The lion and the giant reptiles still lingered smugly in the blood-drenched lake.

They don't need to attack us, thought Fearless bitterly. *That can wait. They're taking this moment to enjoy their triumph. Because Titan has won.*

Keen nudged him. "Come on, Fearless. We must get away from here. I think your baboon friend is at more risk now than ever."

Mud scrambled suddenly up onto Sky's back, hauling himself up by grabbing her ear; she was still too stunned to protest.

"Sky!" he pleaded. "Fearless! I think I know why Dawntrees isn't here!"

CHAPTER SIXTEEN

For a long moment Thorn found himself rooted inside Mud's head, stunned by what had happened. He did not know where his friend's shock and despair ended, and his own began. Staring out through Mud's eyes, he watched Titan's victory, and the panicked stamping and screaming of the herds.

Thorn shook himself loose from Mud's bewildered terror. *How can this have happened?* Rip had been the crocodiles' strong and crafty leader, yet they had turned on him in an instant. And yet, it all made sense. Rend had never been his ally. Even when he approached the bask to outline his plan, even then Titan must have known he was alive.

Peering frantically around, Thorn made the leap to the closest animal: a rat that dodged and scuttled from the hooves of stampeding wildebeests. The thundering vibrations shook his whole body, but as he fled unsteadily through the scratchy

crushed grass, he became aware of another thrumming sensa-
tion: the beat of his tiny heart against his ribs: *My family, my
nest, my pups, I have to get back, get back to them. . . .*

Rip's dead, Thorn tried to remind himself through the fog of
the rat's panic. *I need to find out what went wrong!*

My family! The rat's churning thoughts resurfaced, swamping his own. *My pups! Get back there!*

There was nothing to be learned here; the rat was too
driven by single-minded desperation. Thorn sprang into the
mind of a wildebeest, and he was enveloped in the white dust
that rose from the pounding of his own hooves. *The herd must
stay together. Together!*

Another wildebeest veered, colliding with his shoulder,
making him stumble. . . .

Thorn let himself be thrown from the wildebeest's mind
and into a leopard's. There was rarely an occasion that could
make her panic, but this was just such a calamity. She had risen
to her paws and now stood trembling on the branch where she
had stretched so lazily. *Which way to go?* Titan had eaten leopards before now—or just their hearts. She had no wish to join
her cousins, her spirit trapped in that brute's body forever. She
must calculate the risk, choose a path out of here, and slink
away from Bravelands, never to return. The cubs in her belly
needed a safe territory where they could grow up in peace, and
that meant far from here. . . . Making her decision, leopard-
Thorn sprang lithely down from her branch and slunk toward
the scrubby bushes on the eastern bank of the lake. . . .

Thorn rebounded back into his own body and mind. His

head reeled with the fear of the other animals. No, his eyes had not mistaken him, and this was not some twisted nightmare; Titan had killed Rip, Thorn's most powerful ally, and his scheme was in ruins.

Nut had been right all along; Thorn should never have trusted the crocodiles. This should have been his great moment; he should have been returning to the herds right now as their triumphant leader, their trusted guide, with Titan dragged under the water's surface, never to torment Bravelands again. Instead, all Thorn had achieved was to get Rip killed in the worst of ways. Rip was the only crocodile who had shown loyalty to the Great Spirit. *And he paid with his life. How is that justice?*

As he shook his fur, clinging dizzily to the feeling of his own familiar body, Thorn heard a tremendous, bone-chilling roar split the air. His blood turned cold.

He was used by now to seeing through Mud's eyes; with only a slight jolt, Thorn lurched back into Mud's body. Spinning around to face the lake, he stared in horror.

Titan stood in the shallows, his jaws and mane still dripping dark blood. His eyes glittered, and sun sparked off the golden hairs in his black mane. He was surrounded by grinning wolves.

"You weaklings!" he roared. "You never had a chance against me; what deluded fool told you otherwise?" Titan's glare took in the trembling herds, still milling around and tossing their heads, yet too terrified to flee completely. "Of course you need a strong leader; you've been led until now by fakes and feeble idiots. I, Titan, have come to change all of that. *And you will thank me!*" The lion's glinting eyes narrowed, and his muzzle peeled back from his bloodstained yellow fangs. "Will anyone challenge me? Come forward now—or walk into this water and pledge your allegiance to Titan, best and last leader of Bravelands!"

From across the water came a full-throated roar. "Never!"

Fearless! Thorn-Mud lunged to grab a branch, feeling his heart stutter; it was clear to Thorn, inside his small friend's mind, that Mud's terror for their old friend was just as intense as his own.

"Challenge you?" the young lion went on, ferociously. "Yes. *I* will challenge you, tyrant and heart-thief!"

No! Mud swung around, but there was no time to cry a warning. Fearless bolted toward his enemy, fangs bared. Through Mud's eyes, Thorn saw the charge, but he saw something else too that Fearless did not: Rend the crocodile.

As Fearless's bounding paws touched the water, sending up showers of spray, the huge reptile moved with astonishing speed. Rend twisted and slammed his tail into Fearless's chest, smashing him aside. Fearless was flung across the bank, rolling and crashing against a rock and finally coming to a halt, limp and lifeless.

Thorn gave a high-pitched snarl of fear and anger. Snapping free of Mud's mind and returning to his own, he leaped from his hiding place among the thick foliage. Through the trees he could make out the silver shimmer of the watering hole; it seemed too far away now. *Much too far!* What had he been thinking when he hid himself at this distance? *I have to get there, I have to help. . . .*

Thorn leaped for branch after branch, heedless of the twigs lashing his face. There was only one thing to do now: show himself to the herds, reveal that he was still here and no coward, and rally them all to drive Titan away. *Together we can do it, I know. We* must!

Coiling his muscles to make the jump to the forest floor, Thorn felt something strong catch and snag his ankle. He gasped as he lost his balance and plummeted to the ground.

The air was knocked from his lungs, and he felt as if a buffalo had trampled his ribs. Panting, struggling to rise, Thorn saw paws racing toward him through the bushes.

Lifting his head, he drew back his lips to bare his teeth. There, dashing through the trees, was Viper; behind her ran the Crown Guard, grinning and hooting in triumph.

What? Thorn's heart plummeted. What were these baboons doing here?

Creeper landed far more gracefully than Thorn on the forest litter beside him. The thuggish one-eyed baboon must have ambushed him, Thorn realized—he had grabbed his leg and made him fall.

"Viper! Creeper!" Thorn sucked in a painful breath and staggered to his paws. "I haven't got time for your tricks. I have to get to the watering hole! It's urgent!"

"Oh you do, do you?" Viper smirked. "Another important plan of yours to go wrong, then."

"Leave me be," snarled Thorn, lashing out a paw in Viper's

direction. "Get out of my way! You don't understand, I must go to the lake!"

"It's too late for that," growled a new voice. "Too late already, Baboon."

He knew the voice, and it wasn't one of the Crown Guard. Thorn's fur rose in horror as Menace Titanpride paced through the smirking baboons. The lion cub halted right in front of him.

Gaping at her, Thorn couldn't speak. It seemed impossible. It made no sense—

And then the reality hit him, and a chill surged through his blood. His throat dried like a dead leaf.

"No," he rasped, his voice trembling with rising shock and rage. "You can't. Viper, Creeper—you didn't—"

"Pick the winning side?" Creeper grinned. "Some baboons are smart, Thorn. Smarter than you, it seems."

His words took Thorn's breath away. The Crown Guard were brutes, he knew that—but to side with Titan against all of Bravelands? For a moment Thorn wished he hadn't risen to his paws; his muscles shook, and he felt dizzy with the blow of the betrayal.

"Anyway, most of Bravelands thinks you ran away long ago," Creeper went on, grinning at Thorn. "And Titan would like to keep it that way."

As the one-eyed baboon stalked forward, baring his fangs, Thorn finally found his strength. Clenching his jaws, he rose onto his hind paws to face down Creeper.

"You traitor," he snarled. "Not to me—you've never had

any loyalty to me—but you've betrayed the Great Spirit."

"Great Spirit?" Viper paced forward, a sneer curling her muzzle. "If it exists, it's a useless, weak thing. Such a spirit *deserves* to die. Isn't *that* the way of Bravelands? Your Great Spirit is nothing but a . . . a wounded antelope."

"Bravelands enters a new era today," said Creeper. "By the new Code, *Titan's* Code, the strong and the brave will prosper!"

"You're not strong," hissed Thorn. "You're not brave." He glared around at the Crown Guard. "You're cowards, all of you. Where is Dawntrees Troop? Have you abandoned them? I thought you were supposed to protect them!"

"Dawntrees Troop?" Creeper shrugged and gave Viper a sly grin. He turned back to Thorn. "We couldn't care less."

Then Creeper's grin vanished. "Take him!" he yelled.

Thorn had no time even to defend himself. They leaped on him together, and Thorn found himself pummeled to the ground by muscular arms. Fists smashed into his muzzle and belly, claws dragged on his fur and hide, and he could only curl up helplessly, trying to protect himself and endure the blows.

But there was no escape, not even in complete submission. The big baboons seized his limbs, dragging and stretching them till Thorn was pinioned, spread-eagled on the forest floor.

Great Spirit, help me! Please! His arms and legs felt as if they might pop out of their sockets; the pain was excruciating, but worse was the vulnerability. Thorn had never felt so helpless.

"I'll do it," growled Menace. "It's my right. Father said so."

Padding forward, she stood over him, blotting out the dazzle of the sun through the branches. Menace seemed far bigger than he remembered. He had never thought of the cub as especially dangerous, but oh, she had grown—and there was a very adult coldness in her eyes as they gleamed down at him. When she parted her jaws, he could see that her fangs were more than long enough to rip away his life.

Menace lowered her muzzle close to his ear. Thorn tried not to flinch from her hot breath.

"Father said I can have your heart," she murmured. Her lips curled back, and Thorn could almost feel those savage teeth tearing into his ribcage already. *And there's nothing I can do.*

Abruptly there was a shocked hoot from one of the baboons holding him, and his arm popped free. Thorn had no time to see what had happened. As Menace's jaws lunged for his muzzle, he lashed out with his free arm, tearing his claws wildly across her eyes.

She yowled in pain, staggering back. The baboons holding his other arms and his hind legs let go too, and Thorn scrambled to right himself. There was something in the air all around, black dots that swirled around the Crown Guard and the lion cub, and with it came a noise, an insistent, maddening buzzing. . . .

Bees!

The baboons scattered, yelling and shrieking, and as Thorn blinked hard he saw a bees' nest lying smashed and crumpled on the forest floor nearby. Jerking his head up, he caught sight of Spider, perched in the branches above him. The strange baboon was rocking back and forth, hugging his knees, clearly delighted with his trick.

"Spider!" he yelled.

"Thorn! Get out of there!" Mud's voice reached him across the small glade, and Thorn saw his little friend bounding toward him. At Mud's side, Nut was snatching up rocks and flinging them at the Crown Guard as he ran.

The only sign of Menace was the flick of her tail as she fled into the bushes. Thorn leaped to his feet to dodge the bees, but Spider's aim had been perfect; the insects were fully focused on the Crown Guard, who hopped and screeched and slapped at the swarm around them. Their frantic movements only enraged the bees more. Creeper gave a ragged yell of summons, tearing at his fur, and one by one the Crown Guard staggered after him, diving into the thickest scrub to shake off the bees. It didn't seem to do much good. The bees swirled in a cloud above the scrub, hovering in wait, attacking and driving the baboons back every time a furry head popped up.

At last their agonized yells faded. Thorn could still hear the crash of foliage as Creeper and the rest of the Crown Guard made their escape. Panting, rubbing his sore joints and limbs, Thorn watched Spider jump down from the trees as Mud and Nut ran to join them. Nut was dusting his paws with great satisfaction.

"I whacked that Viper right on the ear with a rock," he said gleefully. "Thorn, are you all right?"

Thorn shook himself, feeling a shiver run through his spine.

"I am now," he muttered. It had been too narrow an escape for comfort, and he could still see the glitter of Menace's eyes as she parted her jaws to crush his head. "Spider, how did you manage to grab that nest? Did you get stung?"

Spider shrugged. "Bees don't hurt Spider, Thorn-friend." He grinned. "*Once*, a bee stung him. When Spider was very little indeed. Ever, ever since, bees have been Spider's friends."

"You have the weirdest friends," said Nut, rolling his eyes and laughing.

"Yup." Spider picked his teeth happily. "And now the bees are the friends of the Great Father too."

CHAPTER SEVENTEEN

Her breath catching raggedly in her dry throat, Sky bolted from her brother's side and thundered to where Fearless lay inert on the hard-packed sand. There was no stir of movement from the lion's limbs, and if his flanks rose and fell, she could not make it out. Surely his ribs were broken at the very least.

"Fearless. Fearless, wake up." Sky nudged her friend urgently but tenderly with her trunk and blew soft breaths at his muzzle. Fear clenched her heart as she saw the blood leaking from his nostrils. The blow from Rend's tail had been savage, and Fearless had hit the rocks hard.

A groan rasped from the lion's throat, and his legs twitched.

"Fearless, don't move. I think you have broken bones." Sky caressed his limbs with her trunk, feeling delicately for any more weaknesses. If Fearless had been mortally injured . . . no, it didn't bear thinking about. And Mud had run off into the woods, and she had no idea what was happening to him, or to the Great Father he had rushed to find. *Everything is falling apart!* From their high hopes as the Great Gathering began, their plans had collapsed into chaos.

Fearless's flanks heaved, and he panted, his eyes flickering open. What mattered right now was that he lived. She lifted her head to stare at the watering hole. Many animals still lingered on the shore, fearful, but more and more of them were wading into the water, trembling, to drink alongside Titan. She could hear their muted, quavering voices, pledging their allegiance and loyalty. It wasn't just the gazelles and the tiny dik-diks; huge buffalo and hippos made their way into the shallows, their eyes wide and staring.

Sky found she couldn't blame the herds. What choice did they have now? They'd seen what happened if they were to defy Titan; even Rip had been mercilessly slaughtered. They were taking what chances they could for survival. And it might buy them some time. At least Titan and his wolves wouldn't kill them right *now*.

Sky turned back to her brother, desperate for reassurance. Buffalo and hippos and leopards might bow before the tyrant—but of all creatures, Boulder was the least likely to submit to the loathsome Titan.

He was deep in conversation with his herd-brothers, but as he caught sight of her he fell silent and raised his head, fanning out his ears. Sky swung her trunk in confusion. That look in his dark gaze: she could not read it. Boulder murmured something to Rock, who gave a slight nod.

Sky didn't want to leave Fearless's side, but she didn't like what she was seeing. Her brother, even Rock, looked defeated. Boulder turned, trudging toward the watering hole, his herd following. His head drooped, though his eyes blazed with resentment.

No! Not Boulder too—

She couldn't bear it. If her brother capitulated to Titan along with all of Bravelands, it truly was over. If Boulder did not have the strength or the courage to withstand the tyrannical lion, no one did.

Boulder came to a halt at the water's edge and raised his head. Sunlight sparked off his tusks; his jaw looked tight, and his eyes were narrow as he glared at Titan. Every animal there fell silent and turned to gape at him.

"For more seasons than I can count," he said, his voice booming across the suddenly still water as creatures paused to watch him, "for rain after dry after rain, as far as I remember and a long way beyond, the elephants have pledged loyalty to the Great Spirit."

Here it comes. Sky felt heartsick, her chest tight and her throat dry.

Her brother took a moment to scan the watering hole and the surrounding herds. "Elephants were often chosen as the Great Spirit's hosts, after all," he went on. "We have long lives, and strength, and great wisdom. We followed the Code, always; we killed only to survive. That was the life and the death we knew in Bravelands, and we did not think to question it." Boulder took a deep ragged breath, and when he spoke again, his voice was wretched. "But all eras end. Even that long and golden season."

Sky's heart tore inside her. She wanted to cry out, she wanted to run to her brother, but her feet stayed rooted to the spot. She had to endure this, she knew. Whatever this was costing Boulder, it was too much. All she could do was endure it with him.

"That age has ended, Titan Wolfpride." Boulder's eyes locked with the black-maned lion's. "It has ended with you. You have killed that season of the life of Bravelands. You have torn down everything we knew. You have smashed the Code as it was. And now we must begin again."

A slow smile curled Titan's muzzle, and he gave a slight nod of acknowledgment.

"And that," Boulder went on, lowering his head so that his tusks scraped across the sand, "that is why the elephants must now break our precious Code." He lifted his head high and spread his ears wide, his eyes blazing. "The Great Spirit must survive. And so, Titan Wolfpride: *you must die.*"

For an instant there was stunned silence, and Sky felt the tiny hairs on her hide rise as a thrill swept through her body. Titan still stared at Boulder, his face suddenly immobile.

Boulder raised his trunk. "For Bravelands and the Spirit!" he trumpeted.

He lurched into a full-on gallop, thundering into the shallows toward Titan. No crocodile would dare to put his body in the way of such a charge. Boulder's brother elephants charged behind him, throwing up such vast fans of spray that for a moment Sky was dazzled by its sunlit glitter.

Animals scattered before the elephants' stampede, bellowing and braying and hooting as they bolted from the lake. Smaller creatures fled from beneath the melee of trampling hooves, tripping and scrambling over one another, squealing in mortal terror. Sky shook herself.

"Nimble! Lively! Get out of here!"

The cheetah cubs needed no second command; they fled up the shore, their black-tipped tails streaking out behind them. Sky had time to puff out a breath of relief before she turned back to the astonishing sight in the lake.

Wolves were scattering before the elephants' onrush, with a panicked shrieking and howling. They scrambled and scratched, snapping their thin jaws at their slower pack members, using their weaker siblings as stepping-stones to bound from the water. Some of the smaller ones disappeared gurgling beneath the water.

Titan himself hesitated, glaring in disbelief at Boulder and his brothers as they stampeded through the water toward him. But his madness hadn't made him stupid. With a roar of fury, he spun around, knocking a last loyal wolf flying. Then he fled, his paws splashing through the water at incredible speed. Whether it was cheetah-spirit driving him or simple fear, Sky could not tell.

It didn't matter. A surge of hope rushed through her, stirring her limbs at last, and with a trumpet of defiance, she launched herself after the other elephants. As she plunged in among the herd, she was quickly swept up in their charge.

Great gray bodies hemmed her in, carried her along, but she wasn't afraid. These were her brother's family, *her* family, her kind. Clenching her jaw in determination, she galloped in their midst, feeling the strength of their righteous anger flowing into her from every side.

She could not see the fleeing Titan, but she knew he was there, just ahead, with the last of his wolves. The angry bellows of the other elephants told her so. The water beneath her feet became hard sand, then gritty earth, as the stampeding herd left the watering hole behind them. Then, abruptly, they plunged into the forest. The elephants ran on, heedless of the snapping, whipping branches; Sky was protected from the worst blows by the elephants around her.

They broke out of the trees, but the elephants did not slacken their chase. Sky could hear the bellowing trumpets of her brother, calling them on, urging them to deliver justice to the foul Titan.

"He won't escape us now, brothers. Take him! Trample the brute under our feet! Crush his worthless flesh! Make his rotten remains feed the earth!"

Sky marveled at the energy that propelled her on. It came from deep within her heart and spirit. This, she knew, could at last be the end of Titan. Giving up now was not an option. As the ground beneath her feet rose in an uphill slope, some of the elephants around her were wearying, their pace slackening. But Sky forged on with the strongest, finding herself closer than ever to the front of the charge.

The noise, the dust, the shaking of the earth were all

overwhelming. With a moment of chilling clarity, Sky knew that she couldn't stop anyway; if she did, she would be trampled herself.

The power of the herd flowed through her, drove her on uphill, leaving forest and grassland behind until the earth dried and paled. It was so hard to see, but the steep rocky path was familiar. She knew this trail so well, and where it led, and her thundering heartbeat jolted.

The Plain of Our Ancestors! Titan was heading for the elephants' most sacred place.

Suddenly her steps were less certain, her feet faltering. Sky gasped for breath, and as one of her feet caught a rock, she almost tripped. Elephants were not meant to run so far, so fast.

But now she *had* to reach the front of the herd. Gathering all her strength and energy, Sky shouldered ahead of the other elephants.

She raised her trunk, blaring out a call of desperation. "Titan must not reach the Plain!"

As her words echoed from cliff to cliff, she caught sight of the black-maned lion cresting the ridge and fleeing within the protecting walls of the sacred plateau. She saw the tails of his remaining wolves flash after him, perhaps twenty or so of the vicious creatures. They vanished from sight within the encircling cliffs.

Boulder was just ahead; with a last spurt of speed, Sky barged against his flank, throwing him momentarily off course. He started and half turned, his racing steps faltering.

Quizzical and perplexed, he shook his head. "We have him, Sky!"

"Boulder, *stop*! You know this is wrong!" She raised her trunk and her voice. *"Look how close we are to the Plain!"*

Slowing, her brother hesitated. Then he stared back at the gap in the cliffs. The elephants behind him halted, milling in frustration, raising their trunks and swinging their tusks.

"Yes," grunted Boulder, his ears spreading wide in anger. "I . . . wasn't paying attention. You're right, Sky."

"This Plain is littered with the bones of our forebears," she reminded the bulls, as an eerie hush fell. "Titan has desecrated it already, simply by entering. We will not do the same."

Some of the males protested, but Boulder silenced them with a snort. "She's right," he said. "We will shed no blood here. We will not disturb our ancestors' resting place."

The bulls lapsed into a sullen mood, scraping at the ground with their feet. Then Boulder flapped his ears, threw up his tusks, and gave a bellow of frustration.

"Titan escapes again!" he cried.

"Titan is safe," rumbled Sky, "within this prison. The walls are sheer, Boulder." She shook her head. "He has not escaped. But this is where our pursuit ends."

"For now, Sky," Boulder corrected her, turning to glare his fury at the entrance to the Plain. *"For now."*

CHAPTER EIGHTEEN

Fearless knew he was awake, but it was as if sleep still held him half in its grip, trying to drag him back to darkness. Was this a dream after all, then? Surely the flames that roared around him weren't real. He could feel their heat, their sharp tongues licking out to burn his flank and belly, but the only light blazing in his aching eyes was sun-dazzle.

He blinked hard. Then again. There was the blurred shoreline, there was the wavering ripple of the water; but where had those running elephants gone?

And . . . where was the fire? *Only within me—*

With a painful effort, Fearless twisted his head. His side looked odd. Wrong. It *felt* wrong.

Everything felt strange and bad: the world, his mind, his body.

Warm breath caressed his muzzle, and Fearless felt the

gentle tickle of whiskers and tongue. That seemed more real than anything; it soothed him, brought him gently back to reality.

"Fearless," urged a voice he recognized as Keen's. "Fearless, you're alive. Thank that Great Spirit of yours."

"Yours, too," mumbled Fearless shakily.

Keen's nod was blurred in his vision. "You're wounded."

"I know it," gasped Fearless as another bolt of pain went through his side.

"The grass-eaters are still in a panic." Keen nodded toward the lake, and Fearless tried to turn his aching head to see. Sure enough, many of the herds still wheeled and galloped, or simply pawed and stamped at the sand, raising their heads to cry out in misery and fear. The shoreline was churned into a chaotic mess of hoof- and pawprints.

Fearless dragged himself up onto his forepaws and narrowed his eyes to try to make sense of the scene. There, visible in glimpses between the frantic animals, lay Rip's mutilated body, his pale belly still exposed to the sun. The corpse was coated in dust from the melee, but the wound was thick with the sticky darkness of congealing blood.

Rip's was not the only lifeless body, Fearless realized with grim satisfaction. Many wolves lay among the trampled animals.

He blinked and angled his head to left and right, staring sharply into the chaos and carnage. *Wolves, but no Titan. Titan still lives. . . .*

Between a stamping, snorting herd of gazelles limped

smaller, furry shadows: four of them. *Thorn and his friends*, thought Fearless, and through the relief, a surge of sudden anger gripped him.

He rose painfully onto all fours. Ignoring the pain that blossomed inside him, Fearless lurched toward the baboons.

As his eyes met Thorn's, the baboon flinched, halted, and backed a step away. "Fearless. You're all right. Thank the—"

"Yes, yes," snarled Fearless. "The Great Spirit has already been thanked, and by lions. Lions who should have been trusted with your plan! Why didn't you confide in me, Thorn? Why didn't you *let me know what was happening?*"

"I . . . it went wrong," stuttered Thorn. "We didn't count on the treachery of the crocodiles. We—"

"Enough!" roared Fearless, and Thorn winced again. His friends too shrank back, though they chittered angrily through bared fangs. "You *knew*, Thorn. You knew I needed to kill Titan, but you took that away from me. And because of your overconfidence, we *both* failed!"

He expected Thorn to rally, to snarl back at him, but the baboon simply looked down at the sand, utterly miserable. "Fearless," he whispered, "I can't deny anything you say. I did fail, and I *should* have trusted you. It's . . . please understand. Listen to me. I'm trying all the time to do what's right—not just for me or for my friends or the other baboons, but for all of Bravelands. That's why I called on Rip and his crocodiles— because I wanted to be sure this would work."

Fearless hesitated. The agony on his old friend's face was almost unbearable to see. *Thorn's tormented by this disaster*, he realized. *And he always will be.*

Thorn sank to a weary crouch, his shoulders hunched. "I ask your forgiveness, my friend. I know it might be too hard to give."

Fearless felt the last of the hot anger seep from his heart. He nodded. Taking a couple of paces toward Thorn, he bent to touch his muzzle to the crown of the baboon's head.

"I forgive you," he said hoarsely. "It's not as if I haven't made mistakes, Thorn."

"*We* do not forgive!" A warthog trotted up, his whiskers bristling as he glared at Thorn. "Easy for you, Lion; the baboon's your friend."

Beside him, all other warthogs snorted in agreement.

"Not our forgiveness!"

"You won't get *that*!"

"Too many of us are dead," squealed a hare, pushing through the gathering crowd toward Thorn. "That's less easy to forget!"

"He's right," neighed a glowering zebra mare.

The dispersed and panicked herds were calming and organizing themselves once again, Fearless saw, but it wasn't in a good way. One by one they approached, some limping, until they formed a deepening host around Thorn and Fearless and the other three baboons.

"Why did you lie, Baboon?" bellowed a hippo from deep in the line. "Why let us think you were dead?"

"Indeed!" yelled a buffalo, and stamped his huge hoof, sending up a cloud of dust. "Explain yourself, *Great Father.*"

Thorn opened his mouth, but he seemed lost for words. A bushbuck lowered his horns menacingly and made as if to butt him from the side. "We needed a Great Father. Needed him more than we ever have. And this—this *coward* pretended to be dead so he could stay out of trouble!"

"That's not what—" began Mud, but he swallowed hard and shut up as the buffalo shoved forward to loom over him.

A leopard prowled through the crowd until she came face-to-face with Thorn. Very deliberately, she licked her jaws. "I knew a baboon was a useless choice as Great Father."

Fearless hastily sidestepped to put himself between her and his friend. "Back off," he growled, "cat-sister."

She glared up at him, moving neither toward Thorn nor back. Three cheetahs stalked forward to stand at her side, their tails switching angrily.

Fearless turned to Thorn. He was all too aware of the weakness of his limbs, the disabling pain in his chest and side, the shaking of his paws. "I'm outnumbered, friend," he growled quietly. "You should leave."

"Yes, you should," grunted the warthog. "Run away, Great Father. Run away *again*."

Thorn cleared his throat, finding his voice at last. He rose onto his hind paws. "I will not," he declared, trembling only slightly. "I've never run away, so why should I start now?"

Almost as one, the angry animals moved forward, tightening their semicircle. From behind Thorn, more of Fearlesspride suddenly moved forward, nodding to Fearless and surrounding Thorn.

"Do not touch the Great Father," snarled Resolute, and Glory growled in agreement.

The hostile creatures halted in astonishment; for the first time since they'd surrounded Thorn, they looked nervous. They exchanged glances, and some began to back away. Only the buffalo and the hippos held their ground.

Two small shadows dodged lithely between the gathered legs and hooves and trotted up to Thorn. Fearless recognized Nimble and Lively, Sky's cheetah cubs.

"We stand with you, Great Father," mewled Nimble, earning a glower from the older members of her kind. Then Resolute and Honor stalked forward too.

Slowly, the angry crowd began to break apart, retreating with muttered threats and venomous glances toward Thorn and his impromptu guard. Tails in the air, the warthogs spun and trotted away haughtily. The zebras broke into a gallop and rejoined their dejected herd. The buffalo snorted a curse and stomped off, kicking up more clouds of dust and sand. The situation was hardly resolved, thought Fearless, but at least any violence had been averted.

"Thank you, Fearless," said Thorn. "And all of you."

Mud blew out a breath of relief. "That could have ended badly if you hadn't been here, Fearlesspride."

Thorn nodded dejectedly, then gave a deep sigh. "I'm grateful for your support, lions of Fearlesspride. More than I can say. But . . . I've lost the rest of Bravelands."

There seemed to be nothing Fearless could say to that; from what he had seen, it was true. As the silence stretched, he shook his mane. Even that small motion sent pain shooting through his chest and flank; it was as if one bone was grinding against the rest. It almost snatched the breath from his lungs.

He swallowed hard, fighting back the agony. "Where do you suppose Titan has gone? Did I see elephants chasing him, or did I imagine that?"

"Oh, they went in pursuit," Nut told him grimly. "But we don't know what happened. With luck they caught him."

"Spider doubts that," said Spider with a shrug.

Fearless gave a rumbling growl deep in his throat. "I don't believe for a moment that Titan's dead."

"I can find out." Thorn padded forward. He sat back on his haunches and closed his eyes. After a moment his face relaxed, looking almost serene. His eyelids flickered.

In the silence, Keen nudged Fearless with his shoulder. "You're in no state to go looking for Titan, let alone fight him."

Fearless took a deep breath, straightening his limbs. He would not let his pain show in his face. Nor would he reveal to Keen just how close he was to collapsing. He gritted his jaws.

"I'm fine," he lied. "I was stunned, that's all. There's nothing wrong with me now."

Keen stared at him for a long time, his penetrating eyes full of concern. But he said nothing more.

Thorn's eyelids flickered again, more rapidly this time, and Fearless was glad of the distraction. The baboon opened his eyes, rubbing his temples hard.

"Was it bad again?" asked Mud.

Thorn shook his head. "I looked through Sky's eyes; that's

not a bad place to be." He smiled slightly. "I have good news and bad news, Fearless. Titan hasn't got away altogether, though they haven't caught him—he's cornered."

"Where?" Fearless felt his heart lurch with urgent excitement. Even that hurt.

Thorn's dark eyes grew very serious. "He's sought refuge on the Plain of Our Ancestors," he muttered. "The elephants are distraught. He has no right to defile that place."

Fearless tensed, though he had to suppress a wince at the pain. "He's trapped there? And the elephants aren't attacking?"

Thorn shook his head. "The elephants won't follow him. It's too precious a place to spill Titan's bad blood; Sky knows it. She's held the bulls back."

"But she won't hold me back," snarled Fearless. "Sky knows I have this right, and it won't be an elephant who spills Titan's blood."

"Fearless!" Keen started forward, his eyes wide with distress.

Fearless turned to him. "You can't stop me," he said softly. "Not this time. You know it."

Keen took a breath. He seemed about to argue, but he shut his jaws and nodded. "Very well, my pride leader." His eyes narrowed. "But we all go with you."

"And so do we," said Nut. "We may not be much help, but we'll be at your side." He grinned. "Time I saw Big Talk turn into Action Lion."

Fearless gave him an affectionate lick on the side of his muzzle.

"Ew," said Nut, wiping it. But he looked pleased.

"All-go-together," sang Spider. "Spider is *very* happy to have lion-friends." He patted the crouching Resolute between the ears; Resolute's eyes started wide. Fearless was amused and relieved when the big lion simply harrumphed in irritation.

"Thank you," Fearless told them all. "It'll be good to have you with me." He began to stride away from the lakeshore, but then turned back for a moment. He gazed at Keen, at Thorn, at Valor.

"But don't forget." He tossed his mane, as proudly as he could. *"Titan is mine."*

CHAPTER NINETEEN

At its highest point, the trail that led to the Plain of Our Ancestors was crowded with elephants, entirely obscuring the gap between the cliffs that led to the plateau. The huge beasts swung their tusks and raked their feet through the gritty white dust; now and again a bull would raise his trunk and trumpet his fury. Bounding between their colossal legs, Thorn did his best to keep up with Fearless, who was loping ahead as quickly as he could. Thorn could not help noticing his bad limp, the slowly clotting blood on his flank and under his nose, and the way his friend winced when a paw hit the ground too hard.

He's in no shape to take on Titan, Thorn thought. He could only hope that Titan was too afraid and unsettled right now to respond to the young lion's challenge. *Stay on the Plain, Titan. For once I want you to hide like the coward you are. . . .*

"Hey!" thundered a bull crossly, as Fearless bumped into

his leg and pushed past. He glared down, but the young lion bounded on.

"Titan is going to pay for all he's done," snarled Fearless, as one by one the elephants turned to stare. "And I'm the one who will make him do it."

A single, huge elephant turned at the head of the pass. He gazed down at the lion loping toward him; instead of shifting, he stepped very deliberately to block his way. Fearless lurched to a halt, breathing hard as he glared at the great bull. Thorn recognized the elephant.

It's Boulder. Sky's brother.

"You go no farther, Lion," rumbled Boulder, lowering his tusks.

Thorn felt a wave of relief. At last, there was someone to say no to Fearless. Boulder would stop his friend getting himself killed.

But to Thorn's astonishment—and quite clearly to Boulder's, too—Fearless squared up to the massive bull, peeling his lips back in a snarl of defiance. "Don't try to stop me."

Boulder's eyes widened in surprise; then he began to swing and toss his trunk. His long tusks gleamed, and his ears flapped wide in threat. A tense hush fell.

This was not going to end well. Thorn had seen in the past what a full-grown bull could do to a lion. Fearless wouldn't stand a chance if Boulder put those feet and tusks to use.

There was rumbling and shuffling in the elephants' ranks. Some glanced over their shoulders and shifted aside, and Thorn saw Sky step forward between the two antagonists.

She glared at her brother, then turned to the lion.

"You don't understand, Fearless." Sky's voice was quiet, but clear and full of authority. "Boulder cannot let you enter the Plain of Our Ancestors. It's a sacred place to us, and blood cannot stain the ground there. It's bad enough that Titan is already fouling it with his presence."

Thorn eyed Fearless, feeling a sick nervousness in his belly. It was quite obvious that his friend was battling pain; Thorn could see it in the tension of his muscles and the trembling of his jaw. But the lion's eyes were full of vengeful fire, and Thorn had a feeling that if not for his injury, Fearless might have flung himself at Boulder. The elephants were silent, staring at Fearless, and Sky's ears twitched.

The standoff was shattered as a mocking hoot sounded from the ridge above them. Every creature turned to stare up.

A twisted, windswept old juniper grew at the edge of the cliff; in its branches hunched an ugly, one-eyed baboon, his fur patchy and ravaged with red scars.

"Creeper!" Thorn rose onto his hind paws, glowering up at the baboon.

Creeper peeled back his lips and gave a screech of contempt. "Thorn *Greatfather*, huh?" He lifted his fist. In it he clenched a long, curved bone, bleached by the sun. Sky gave a gasp of distress and trotted a few steps up the trail.

"That bone belongs to our ancestors," she cried. "Leave this place. Now!"

In response Creeper only laughed harder and tossed the bone from paw to paw. "This is no longer the Plain of your pathetic Ancestors. It's the den of Titan Wolfpride, and a fine den it is too!"

A rumble of fury rose from the assembled elephants. Rock gave a trumpet of rage, and Boulder raked the stony ground with his foot.

"You won't come in, will you?" jeered Creeper. He flipped the bone, catching it just before it could clatter to the ground. "Is it because it's your holy place? Or is it just that you're all scared of Titan? Don't worry, poor little elephants. Titan won't hurt you, and he won't even gnaw on any more of your grandfathers." The baboon put a finger thoughtfully to his jaw. "Well. Not if you give him a sacrifice."

"You will regret this, intruder," bellowed Rock.

"Sacrifice?" seethed Sky. "What do you mean?"

"Oh, it's not much. Not much *at all*. Such a little, insignificant thing, though he *thinks* himself the most important creature in all of Bravelands." Creeper picked his teeth and swung the bone carelessly in his fist. "Give us Thorn."

Mud gave an indignant shout; Nut a derisive laugh. Sky swiveled her head toward Thorn and shook it slightly.

"We will not give you up to this impudent baboon," she told him, her eyes sparking with anger.

"I would if I were you," sang Creeper. "Titan is tired of your Great-Father-Monkey and his tricks. If Thorn doesn't give himself up, Titan won't ever leave your precious graveyard. You know, the wolves need to keep their teeth sharp, and this place is very helpful. I daresay it'll take them a long time to grind so many bones to dust, but eventually they will.

Maybe they'll leave after that? I don't know, it's such a nice view from up here. Maybe Titan and the Wolfpride will stay *forever*." His eyes glinted bright with malice.

Thorn watched Sky as she glared helplessly up at Creeper. Her face was tormented; she looked as if she didn't know whether to weep or rage or sink to her knees in despair.

Thorn turned to his friends. "I have no choice," he said quietly. "I cannot let them do this."

"Thorn, no!" cried Mud.

"I agree with Mud," said Nut. "Don't you dare, Thorn!"

"Spider thinks this would be the stupidest thing *ever*," said Spider, tickling his lizard's throat.

Truth to tell, Thorn thought the same. It *was* a stupid notion. *I'm going to die if I go in there.*

But how could he let Sky down? How could he disappoint the Great Spirit? Maybe this was what he'd been meant to do all along.

"I can't let those brutes desecrate the Plain of Our Ancestors," said Thorn. His head sagged. "I'll go with Creeper. I—"

"*We reject your terms!*"

Sky's furious bellow made Thorn jump. He gaped at her in astonishment. The young elephant raked the ground with her tusks, her eyes blazing. "You've crossed a line, Creeper Blackheart. You may not threaten us! Rock is right." She nodded at her betrothed, and her voice was deadly. "You will regret what you've done today."

Creeper tilted his head. He stared down at her for a long moment.

"Very well," he growled at last. "Let your bones be cursed then. Or rather, the bones of your ancestors." Springing down from his perch, he vanished between the rocks and into the plateau.

Thorn shook himself. He could not let the baboon out of his sight. Clenching his jaws, he flung his mind forward, seeking out his enemy and plunging into the dark and hateful clouds of Creeper's consciousness.

He was racing back across the plateau, the piece of rib bone still gripped in his paw. His casual mockery of the elephants had been nothing but an act; it was hot anger that roiled in his chest and gut.

Thorn won't get out of this so easily; Titan will see to that. And then the baboons will be rid of that arrogant, self-righteous troublemaker forever.

He leaped over another pile of bleaching bones, scrambled over a broken skull. Thumping to the ground, he scratched at his raw hide. It maddened him that Thorn and his cronies had tricked them with a bees' nest.

Vicious, spiteful Thorn: oh, he'll be sorry he ever thwarted me.

When he took Thorn's head back to Dawntrees, the troop would thank him. And they'd beg for a Crownleaf: Creeper Crownleaf.

No more of that council nonsense, no more equal leadership. It's all ver-vet-dung.

The Crown Guard would serve him, and they'd do it happily. Once he was rid of Thorn, and Titan ruled Bravelands . . .

A few wolves sprawled in the stubby dry grass ahead, chewing on bones; their big ears twitched, and they gave him dismissive glances as Creeper dodged through them. His paws hurt. His skin hurt. Bees! Fire! Oh, he'd tear Thorn's throat out slowly. . . .

Titan lay on a flat white rock in the middle of the plateau, his annoying daughter at his side. Nearby sat the other Crown Guard baboons, picking and scratching grumpily at their own bee stings. As Creeper approached, Titan lifted his black-maned head and showed his fangs. Creeper slowed, bowing his head, catching his breath, and finding a respectful tone.

"Why are you here, Baboon?" growled Titan.

"They refused!" panted Creeper. "They wouldn't give up the Great Father." He snorted and spat.

"I can see that for myself," drawled Titan, licking his jaws. "You're alone. So I'll ask again. Why are you here?"

Creeper opened his mouth to explain once more, but his words dried in his throat. There was something in Titan's eyes that he didn't like.

Menace sat up, tilting her head to peer at him curiously. "Are you going to explain, Creeper? My daddy said you weren't to come back without Thorn."

"But I tried," Creeper blurted, feeling the first stirrings of real fear. "It's not as if I could force them! I came back straight away, Titan. I knew you'd want to know. I knew you'd want to do something about those impudent animals."

"Yes." Titan sat up on his haunches and shook his mane. "Impudent animals. I can't tolerate impudence . . . or failure. I've given you two commands, and you've failed me in both." He licked his jaws. "If that isn't impudence, what is?"

Creeper swallowed. He glanced from one side to the other, then back at the two lions. *No. Titan's bluffing. He needs me.*

Menace nodded slowly. Her jaws parted a little, and she breathed faster; Creeper could distinctly see the gleam of her fangs.

Creeper glanced at his Crown Guard comrades; they looked nervous. Viper backed away, as if she was trying to conceal herself behind the others. There would be no help from those so-called friends.

"I'll make this right, Titan," blurted Creeper, turning back to Titan. "I'll bring Thorn back myself if I have to!"

"That was the original idea." Titan yawned, his fangs and his black throat showing. "I'm not keen on second chances."

"Generous Titan," hissed a voice behind Creeper. "Benevolent Titan."

Creeper started and spun around. Silent, unnoticed, the wolf pack had formed into a group behind him. He had nowhere to run. Panic clenched his chest.

"Your heart, Creeper," mused Titan. "I think perhaps it's dry and wizened, with little spirit left." He turned to cock his head indulgently at his eager, slavering daughter. "But it'll do."

"Titan, no!" The time for pleading was over; Creeper knew he could only scream and beg. "No, I—"

His voice and breath were knocked from him as the wolves sprang. He felt a terrible, ripping agony, heard the crunch of his own bones, knew the most absolute and despairing of terror, and—

Thorn drew away with a lurch of his mind, scrabbling

desperately to leave Creeper. He found himself, panting, with the elephants once more.

"Thorn? Thorn!" Sky stood over him, her trunk-tip touching him gently. Mud and Nut and Spider were gathered around, their eyes full of concern.

"What happened?" Mud clutched his arm. "Thorn, what did you see?"

Thorn could still feel the bite of those savage fangs, the hot breath of death, the unbearable knowledge of his coming demise. In his Thorn-self, he felt a surprising sadness for the baboon who had once been his troop-mate. He shook himself violently.

"Creeper is dead," he said, hoarsely.

His friends fell silent. Mud put his hands over his mouth. Nut made a disgusted face.

"Oh dear," said Spider, quite happily.

Thorn gathered his breath and his composure. "Sky . . . There's something more important." He laid his paw on her trunk. "Titan has already started to desecrate the dead."

"I'll go in there. Don't try to stop me." Fearless limped between Nut and Mud, his eyes hard. "Listen to me, all of you. He must die. *Now*. And I am the lion to do this. Titan has already turned the crocodiles, and *some* baboons"—he gave Thorn a respectful nod—"and even the herds are submitting to him. They're scared of him, and they're right. We have to deal with this threat to Bravelands now—or never."

Thorn reached out to stroke his friend's muzzle. A memory came back to him with a bittersweet pang: *That first time Fearless let me stroke his muzzle* . . . He'd been only a little cub, nervous but brave, surrounded by a troop of baboons—half of whom had wanted to eat him. But the rest had cooed over the adorable baby lion, had agreed readily to Stinger's proposal: *Brightforest Troop will have a grown lion of our own one day! Imagine, my friends!*

Thorn had stepped cautiously forward through the curious ranks, had reached out a paw to the scared little cub. He remembered how his paw had shaken, how his heart had raced. But when he'd touched the lion's nose, it had been softer than he'd expected. Big brown eyes had gazed into his, suspicion melting into anxious trust. *And the Cub of the Stars licked my paw. . . .*

Those fangs of Fearless's had been small, then. Now they were long, and sharp, and deadly. His eyes were older, fiercer, lit by the dark flame of experience. This young lion's heart was ablaze with righteous vengeance.

But he was hurt, and Thorn had a feeling he was hurt *badly*.

"You're right, Fearless," he said at last. "But . . ." He drew a deep breath and glanced around at the elephants. Weren't they famously wise? Perhaps they knew some way to save his friend . . . some way to level the odds . . .

There, at Sky's side, stood Rock, her staunch, courageous betrothed. That elephant had literally walked through flames to rescue the animals of Bravelands, and Rock was a true friend of the Great Spirit. The evidence was there, in the still-raw scars and patches on his dark hide.

"Fire," said Thorn suddenly.

"What?" Sky blinked.

"Fire will drive Titan out. Out of the Plain, and out of Bravelands." Thorn smiled at Spider. "Fire will help us this time, not harm us."

"Now wait a minute." Boulder barged forward. "Fire is not something to be treated lightly, Thorn."

"No," said Sky firmly. "And I'm sorry, Thorn, but you cannot bring flames to the Plain of Our Ancestors. The destruction would be worse than anything Titan and his wolves can inflict."

"Not on the Plain itself," said Thorn, touching her trunk again. "Remember the smoke? Remember how it drove every creature before it, whether weak and small or powerful and huge? We will build fires *around* the Plain. Starting here, at its entrance. Fear and smoke will drive out Titan and his wolves, long before the bones are burned."

Sky glanced at Rock, then at Boulder; then she turned her agonized gaze toward the Plain. She swung her trunk in confusion. "I don't know. It seems far too risky."

"The fire in the forest," said Rock, "it wasn't a thing you could control. It went where it willed."

"True," rumbled Boulder. "We cannot control what the fire-flowers do once they bloom. The danger is too uncertain."

"Rock-friend isn't correct," said Spider suddenly and politely. "Fire doesn't go where it wills." He smiled up at Sky, letting his agama lizard scuttle around his neck.

They all stared at him, surprised. Thorn frowned.

"Fire," added Spider, "goes where the food is."

"What?" said Boulder, looking genuinely bewildered.

"He's right," said Thorn, excitement rising inside him. "Spider's seen more fire than any of us; he *makes* it."

"He does?" Rock blinked and peered down at Spider with a new and nervous respect.

"Spider's the one who showed us how to make a fire-break," Thorn explained. "He told me the fire-flowers follow what they eat. I didn't believe him then, but he was exactly right. The fire couldn't cross a place if there was nothing for it to burn."

Sky flapped her ears. "I think . . . perhaps this could work after all," she said eagerly. "Boulder, remember how we cleared the fire's path to stop it, after Thorn told us what to do?"

"It was Spider who explained it to me," put in Thorn, and Spider puffed out his chest.

Sky turned hopefully to her brother. "There's not much to burn in the center of the Plain—except for bones, that is, and the flowers needn't ever get near those."

Spider nodded in satisfaction. "Bones do not burn. Nothing for the flowers to eat. A bit of grass, is all. Put out food for the fire around the edge, and that's where it will stay."

"I still say it's dangerous," grunted Boulder, "but perhaps it's worth a try. If what Thorn and Spider say is true . . ."

"It's true." Thorn tilted his head to scan the sky for birds. A single eagle soared high over the ravine, and he cupped his paws to his muzzle to call it down.

"Air-flier! Wing-spreader! Cloud-breacher! Come to me!"

Tilting its feather-tips, the eagle adjusted the angle of its wings. Its flight path dipped, and it flew lower, lower, till

Thorn could make out its black, determined eye.

"My friend," he cried.

"Great Father." The eagle dipped its head a little. Its Sky-tongue was surprisingly shrill, like its hunting cry. "How can I be of service on this fine blue day?"

"I thank you, brother bird." Thorn smiled up. "Bring others—vultures, buzzards, hornbills, weavers. Bring them all! We need you—we need brushwood. Bring twigs and branches, dead bush and scrub. A few dry leaves, if the bulbuls and sparrows will carry them!"

The eagle had a light of perplexed amusement in its eye. "And where shall we bring all this, Great Father?"

"To the edges of the plateau," Thorn told him. "Drop it in great piles all around the border of the Plain. We will do the rest!"

"Very well. The Great Father's wisdom is mysterious, but it is always wisdom." With a last nod, the eagle soared into the sky, then flew down toward the sprawling savannah at the foot of the mountain. Thorn saw a flock of blue starlings rise from the trees, and a buzzard take off from its nest, as they flew to join the eagle.

His friends were staring at him, as always, in astonished respect; none more so than the elephants who had not witnessed this before. Thorn closed his eyes, his heart beating thunderously within his rib cage.

And now, all we can do is wait.

CHAPTER TWENTY

Against the glare of the sinking sun, and the streaks of golden cloud across the violet horizon, Sky could make out black dots. She blinked. The birds were approaching rapidly, and soon she could make out each bird kind: hornbills and storks, shrikes and doves and marsh harriers, hawks and egrets and weaverbirds. She had never seen so many birds in the air, even at the grandest of Gatherings. *The birds respect and trust Thorn*, she thought. *They know he is a fine Great Father.*

But of course, it wasn't only Thorn they trusted. The birds, more than any other Bravelands creature, knew the power of the Great Spirit—and that power could bring them together.

Tearing her eyes away from the vast flocks, Sky peered around the edges of the Plain. The shadows beneath the rock faces were long now, and deepest purple, but she could make out the positions of most of the elephants and lions. Boulder and his brothers, convinced by Thorn's plan, had finally allowed the lions to pass through the entrance onto the borders of the vast plateau, but none of them had ventured to its interior. That was still held by Titan, his wolfpride, and his baboon allies. The baboons must be afraid now, since Creeper's violent death; Sky could only imagine how badly the surviving Crown Guard wanted to get out of there. Even for Creeper, she could not help feeling a twinge of pity.

But they brought it on themselves.

Titan and his wolfpride must have known what was happening at the edges of their temporary territory, but no shadow stirred, no creature emerged from that central ground. Titan must have been caught off guard by this strategy of Thorn's; otherwise, Sky knew, she would already see him directing the wolves in a sneaky counterattack or summoning some other terrified and enthralled creatures to his aid. Titan was now on the defensive, at least—and after the debacle at the watering hole, that gave Sky a thrill of satisfaction.

Cries and screeches and whistles echoed in the air above her, and she glanced up again. The birds were overhead now, and they had done as Thorn asked. Eagles carried broken and torn branches; a big hornbill bore a thin bleached stump; the sparrows and weaverbirds and starlings brought leaves and twigs and grass, and the tiniest scraps of forest litter. Each bird alone could never have made a difference, but together they were depositing great piles of dry brushwood at regular points against the encircling cliffs. *So many birds*, Sky thought in amazement. The high clouds were still stained with the purples and pinks of sunset, but the colors were almost blotted out by the black mass of the gathered flocks. Already twilight felt like night.

Fearlesspride waited by the plateau's entrance, not far away, but Sky wasn't watching them. Near her feet, in the patch of sunlight on the border, Spider crouched over a small heap of dry leaves and grass. She turned her attention to him, fascinated, reaching out her trunk to sniff at his little stack of tinder, and at the sparkling-clear piece of stone he cupped in his paws.

"The Plain's gate is at the west," he told his lizard. "That's lucky, see. So we get all the sun that's left. Spider hopes it's enough."

He watched the vast crowd of birds as they dropped their last scraps of wood and bark, then rose into the air and flew back beyond the cliffs. With satisfaction, he nodded.

"Spider reckons that'll do," he muttered. "Good birds. Just in time, eh?"

He gripped the stone carefully between his fingers and frowned at the horizon. The setting sun's light was very intense now, blazing between thin golden clouds and painting the shadows of the animals far across the Plain beyond.

"Still warmth in it," Spider grunted, and angled his stone with great care into the rays.

The dazzle was unexpected. Sky had to blink hard as he twisted the stone, focusing the splayed sunlight into a single brilliant beam. For what seemed a breathless age, Spider crouched there immobile, the shard of intense sun-glow aimed at the curled dry leaves before him.

Sky saw his head twist; he was glancing anxiously at the horizon again. Far across the savannah, the sun was sinking fast. Spider's paws trembled a little, but the beam itself held steady. To Sky's eyes, it seemed more brilliant and red-gold than before.

"Come on, brother-Sun," Spider muttered. "Come along, now. Don't say good night just yet."

The lowest rim of the blazing sun touched the Plain on the far western horizon. Without even understanding what was happening, Sky felt her chest clench with anxiety. In her head she chanted along with Spider's mumblings: *Don't go, brother-Sun. Don't go yet.* . . .

An acrid tang drifted to her trunk, and she started. Staring down at the dry leaves, she saw a wisp of pale smoke shimmer out of the heap.

Spider grinned. The pile was smoldering now, the smoke snaking out in darker, thicker coils. Spider dipped his head and seemed to coax the flame by talking to it. As Sky watched in fearful fascination, a fire-flower bloomed, sudden and beautiful.

Some primitive instinct sent her stumbling back in gut-deep horror as the flames blossomed and grew, young and hungry. Spider tossed down his stone and clapped his paws together. Then, turning, he shaded his eyes at the last intense glow of the sun.

"Thank you," he hooted. "Sleep now, brother-Sun."

And the glow beyond the far plains blinked out and died.

The air was instantly darker violet, its clouds streaked pink-gold, but its beauty wasn't what fascinated Sky. In the swiftly deepening dusk, the flames were taking hold of Spider's tinder. They crackled and hissed, devouring the little stack rapidly.

The fire goes where the food is, Sky remembered. Curling her trunk carefully around a burning twig, she pressed it closer into the larger heap of leaves and brushwood. For a heart-stopping moment she thought it wouldn't catch; then the flame danced higher and roared up a dead pine branch.

The pile was alight! She could hear the low snarl of the flames as they intensified in the heart of the deadwood. Spider grabbed a burning branch and bounded toward Nut at the next woodpile.

Snatching the branch, Nut pushed it hard into that heap. It caught in moments, the flames seeming to take no more than a breath before erupting through the heart of the brushwood. Already smoke was billowing up the cliffs and drifting across the Plain, but there was little to attract the flames themselves in the wasteland of stunted grass. A burning branch in his own paw, Nut sprinted toward Boulder, who waited with his trunk impatiently extended.

Sky held her breath as one baboon, one elephant after another, lit a lengthening line of fires around the circle of the Plain. One by one, the heaps of dry wood burst into golden flame, and the roar and reek of the inferno filled the plateau before even half the fires were lit. Once again, that spurt of instinct twisted in her belly: this was wrong, dangerous. *I should run.* Flames rose to lick the sky—if they reach the clouds, would they in turn burst into flame?

No. I trust Great Father Thorn. Summoning her courage, she turned her head to peer through the smoke toward the center of the Plain. Nothing could be seen, not yet. But it could not be other than terrifying to see those fires spring into life on every side.

She imagined Titan, rising to his paws with Menace. She could picture the two lions, with their wolves and the baboon Crown Guard, backing toward safety on the far side of the plateau. But there, too, Sky realized that fires were now erupting, and the still air was soon thick with smoke from all directions. *There will be no escape, Titan Wolfpride.* Sky felt a flicker of thrilling certainty. This was truly going to work! *Where else can Titan go?*

A few blades of grass burst into small fire-flowers at Sky's feet. Hurriedly she stamped them out, feeling the heat even through her thick pads of skin. *The flames must not reach the bones of our Ancestors.* Through the thickening smoke she saw other elephants doing the same, crushing the fire-flowers that crept from the edges of the brushwood stacks. It was clear the fire was giving up that route willingly; what was charred and trampled grass when there was so much food for its flames in the brush piles themselves?

Clever Spider, thought Sky, tears stinging her eyes.

The elephants, together with Thorn, Mud, Nut, and Spider, were already making their rapid way back around the cliffs toward the plateau entrance that Spider called the

"Gate." When they were all assembled, they turned to watch the smoke-shrouded Plain, but by now there was nothing to be seen in the murky darkness. The only sound was the hungry crackle of fire-flowers, and from somewhere deep within the plateau, guttural grunts, choking coughs, and hoarse howls of fear.

Thin, sinuous shapes rushed out of the smoke with a suddenness that took Sky aback; the wolves were fleeing. An elephant lifted his foot to stamp on the leader, but it dodged nimbly and shot past.

"Never mind the wolves," growled Fearless, who had come to stand next to Sky. "Let their worthless hides go. It's their leader I want."

"He's right," Sky told the elephants, and Rock nodded. "Keep on the alert for Titan."

"Are the fire-flowers dying?" asked a young bull, Ravine. He scraped the ground anxiously.

"They mustn't," said Thorn grimly. He glanced up at the sky, then grinned. "But my friends know what to do."

The birds were returning. Once again they carried branches, twigs, and bark; once again they dropped their burdens around the edge of the Plain, feeding the ravenous flames. The fire roared back to life. Night had fallen completely, but eerie shapes were visible now, jutting from the heart of the Plain, outlined in firelight: gigantic skulls, jagged ribs, great spears of tusk, all lit by a violent orange glow. Sky's breath caught in her throat. *The bones are not for you, fire-flowers!*

But though smoke swirled and twisted between the ancient

bones, no flames leaped to attack them; no skeletons erupted in fire, no tusks smoldered and blackened in the heat. Closing her eyes, Sky gave silent inward thanks to the Great Spirit.

When she opened her eyes once more, living shapes were moving in the sinister glare. Her eyes streamed and an acrid tang stung her sensitive trunk, but she made herself peer harder. Now she saw them clearly: wolf after wolf, bolting from the dense smoke. One by one they fled, skinny shapes that flashed past the waiting elephants and vanished into the darkness. No black-maned lion loomed from the murk, but Sky thought she could hear something, deep within the circle of cliffs: an enraged roaring that made the smoky air shiver.

Could it be the flames? No. It sounded different from the fire's voice, she thought with an inward shudder. There was a distinct note of darkness and evil in the muffled sound.

Two more wolves. Three. A cluster of five. Two Crown Guard baboons; she didn't recognize them, but then they seemed diminished and pathetic as they fled. They too disappeared into the darkness of the Bravelands night. Neither of them was Thorn's sworn enemy, Viper: Sky was sure of that.

A limping wolf, its fur burned and torn. And then another, barely able to drag itself through the gate of the Plain. As it lurched down the trail, Sky thought she heard its last whimper, swiftly cut off. Most likely, its friends had put it out of its final misery.

After that, no further creature appeared. The air was bad enough where Sky stood, scorching her throat and choking her trunk; surely any creature left on the Plain must have succumbed to the suffocating smoke? There was nothing to do now but wait silently in the night, the hearts of baboons and lions and elephants beating alike. There was something so terrible and beautiful about the circle of fire that raged around the Plain of Our Ancestors.

As the night drew on, stars appeared now and then, twinkling through the pall of smoke; but then the birds would reappear, bringing their inexhaustible supply of food for the flames, keeping the fire flourishing at the edges of the plateau.

It was hard to track the progress of the night hours, with the stars and moon mostly invisible. But eventually the fires began to subside. The exhausted birds were at last running out of brushwood and branches; or perhaps they were simply returning to roosts that had been left too long. The flocks' numbers gradually dwindled until only the eagle was left, soaring on the disturbed air currents above the Plain. He stooped, tipping his wings in salute to Great Father Thorn, then soared away out of sight beyond the cliffs.

A bone-deep weariness stole across Sky's limbs quite suddenly. She blinked and swayed; the smoke wasn't as thick now, drifting into ragged tendrils, and through the murk it was clear that day was breaking. The sky had paled to lilac-gray, and beyond the far cliffs, a pale shimmer of gold outlined the eastern mountains.

"He's dead." Nut's voice broke the silence. "He can't have survived that."

"I'd hope not," grunted Boulder.

Sky peered through stinging eyes toward the clearing Plain. The wood stacks were almost burned out, blackened and scattered and smoldering. Wisps of feeble smoke licked the nearest grass, but the elephants had done their job well at the beginning of the night; there was nothing to catch those dying flames in the charred, trampled grass around the fires. Already the thick smoke seemed more like a tattered morning mist. *If it wasn't for the stink of death and burning*, thought Sky with a shiver along her spine.

She raised her head and looked east. Spider's "brother-Sun" burst like a new flame at the horizon, spilling rays across the center of the plateau, turning the remaining smoke to golden mist. Sky gasped at its beauty.

Then, as the sun rose, a roar echoed out from the very heart of the Plain, savage and defiant and unforgiving.

And alive.

Sky's blood ran cold as a river. Around her, the elephants stiffened, lifting trunks to scent the air. Mud chittered in distress.

"How?" bellowed Boulder. *"How?"*

Fearless struck the earth with a paw, raking his claws deep into the grass. He gave a furious snarl—but Sky thought she heard something else in it. Satisfaction, maybe.

"And now, he's mine," growled Fearless. "There's nothing more you can do. You've stripped him of his wolfpride. It's my turn."

"You can't," snapped Keen, padding to his side. "You're not in any state to take him on."

"I agree with the rangy lion," said Rock. "Don't be a fool, Fearless. Titan's defeated now. There will be other moments."

"None like this one," said Fearless. "He's weakened and alone. And trapped." His eyes glinted with determination.

"Fearless, please." Thorn raked a paw through his mane. "There's no sense in doing this now, old friend. You know you're hurt!"

"No sense?" bellowed Boulder. "He's a suicidal idiot if he does this now."

Sky backed away, distressed. She did not want to see Fearless fight, not right now, not in his state of injury. But nor did she want any part of what seemed about to become a rancorous squabble. And somewhere deep inside, she felt a qualm of uncertainty. *Titan is still alive, and Fearless could be right. There may never be another chance. Titan might slip away somehow. He might recover, regroup, return. . . .*

Turning her head, she stared into the drifting pall of sun-gilded smoke. She sucked in a wondering breath. With a glance to left and right, she realized no other creature saw what she was seeing.

But it was no illusion. Perhaps this vision was for her alone—but she was not imagining that those coils of smoke were coalescing, shaping themselves into a familiar figure. It was one Sky had seen before, in the morning mist after the Great Battle against Stinger. A massive, imposing, but beloved elephant matriarch, her ears spread wide, her tusks glinting gold in the dawn.

"Great Mother," whispered Sky. She lurched forward a step, lowered her head.

The smoke-form of the great old elephant moved toward Sky; her eyes were as golden as the sun, yet they were gentle and kind.

Sky. A beloved voice, unheard for far too long, echoed inside her head. *Let the lion enter the Plain. Let him do what he must. He has earned this.*

Sky gazed at her beloved grandmother, her heart almost bursting. "But your bones, and the bones of our ancestors—if blood is spilled, and it will be—"

Sky. Great Mother's voice was so warm. *It's no longer the time to protect the dead. Now you must protect the living.*

A whisper of breeze touched Sky's ears, and the acrid air stung her eyes. She blinked hard, and when she looked once more, the trails of smoke had dissipated. Great Mother's golden form had vanished.

There was no time to mourn all over again, and Sky could not bear to. She turned sharply to Boulder and Rock.

"Let Fearless enter," she commanded, raising her head and spreading her ears wide. "Step aside, brothers." Great Mother's soft words came back to her. *And let him do what he must.*

Boulder opened his mouth as if to protest, but closed it again when his gaze met hers. Rock simply watched her with warmth and gave her a slight nod. The other elephants, one by one, stepped back from Fearless.

His mane glinted gold in the dawn light, and his eyes

burned with longing. Beneath his sleek tawny fur, his muscles rippled. But there were scratches and lesions on his hide, and dark blood stained his pelt. He seemed to have aged a year in just the last day.

Keen gave a single, tormented growl; then he fell silent. Thorn looked stunned.

"Go, Fearless," Sky said quietly.

Gazing at her, he nodded.

"Come what may, Sky Strider," he said, "I will fulfill my oath."

CHAPTER TWENTY-ONE

It all came to this. Every moment since he had watched Gallant die at the claws of Titan; everything he had done or said, every decision he had made, had brought him to this moment. Though he was afraid, he was calm too. The promise he had made to avenge Gallant had filled his dreams and waking life for so long. No, he simply wanted it to be done with.

Fearless stood in the first golden light of the new sun, letting its warmth flow into him.

I will keep my promise to my lost family. Come what may.

"Remember, my father is cunning." Ruthless was at his side; Fearless glanced at him. Why was he so surprised at how the cub had grown? Already tufts of black-and-gold fur fringed his neck and head; his mane was coming in far sooner than Fearless's had. One day he was going to be a fine, strong lion. Fearless smiled at him.

"I won't forget, Ruthless."

"Watch for attacks from all your sides at once." The cub stared at him pleadingly. "Be ready for the unexpected, at any moment."

"I'll try to do the impossible." Fearless laughed. "Don't I always, Ruthless?"

"Listen to the cub, and don't joke," growled Valor. "You know what Titan is. I lost my father and my mate to that brute in there; I don't want to lose my brother too."

"Don't even say that, Valor." Keen nudged her, then nuzzled Fearless's neck. "I have faith in you, my friend," he said, a little too eagerly. "I know you'll beat Titan. But take me with you. I can watch your back, look out for Titan's tricks."

"I can't let you do that, Keen." Fearless pressed his face to his friend's. "The oath is mine alone to keep."

"Fearless." He felt a paw on his shoulder, and turned to see Thorn's face, creased with concern. "My friend. Mud is reading his stones for you. It might help with those . . . those unexpected moments, as Ruthless called them." Thorn gave a twisted smile and pointed to his small friend, who was already scattering his stones close by, in the shadows of the cliff.

"All right," said Fearless gruffly. He butted Thorn gently with his head. "Let Mud tell me what he sees."

Mud did not glance up at Thorn or Fearless. He was watching the shadow withdraw with the rising sun, his face intent as its line crept back and back to illuminate each stone in turn. Fearless had never understood how Mud could see the things he saw in them. He swallowed hard, wondering what the little baboon would tell him.

Though it didn't matter, in the end. This battle had to be fought. *Come what may.*

Together they watched Mud reach out to touch his stones, turning, adjusting, frowning.

"Believe me, Fearless," murmured Thorn, "the Great Spirit is with you."

"I'm sure of it," growled Fearless.

"Good." Thorn patted his mane and left his fingers there for a moment, twined in Fearless's fur. "Good."

Mud glanced up. "Thorn. Fearless." His eyes were unreadable, but his mouth twitched with nerves.

"What do you see, Mud?" asked Thorn.

"It's . . ." Mud glanced back at the stones. "It's not very clear." He chewed his lip and swallowed. "It . . . it's hard to say."

Fearless watched the little baboon. He seemed to be staring very hard at the stones, as if it was an excuse not to look at Thorn and Fearless.

"I'm not afraid," said Fearless.

Even as he said it, he knew it wasn't true. *I am afraid, Father Gallant. I'm sorry. I'm sorry I've let you down.* A tiny ember of resentment flared inside him. *Why give me a name I couldn't live up to? Why?*

The spark of anger flickered out as quickly as it had risen, and a quiet calmness settled on him. *Because you knew, Father, didn't you? You knew that even in the worst moments, even if I failed, I'd try to live up to it.*

"It's all right, Mud," he said more calmly. "If it's bad, you can tell me."

Mud's head jerked up again, and this time Fearless could see the anguish in his face. "I'm sorry, I can't. It's too confused. The stones—they're like that sometimes." His voice faded.

Fearless licked the top of Mud's head. "Don't worry, old friend. Today Titan's reign of terror ends. I promise you."

"I know it will." Mud's throat sounded constricted. "The Great Spirit go with you, Fearless."

There was nothing left to do, no more words of advice to take. Fearless was on his own in this confrontation, as he'd always known he must be. Taking a deep breath, he stiffened his aching muscles, turned, and strode toward the center of the Plain. His pride, his baboon friends, and the elephants were watching his every move; he could feel it. But they remained absolutely silent.

Smoke still drifted in tendrils and billows, obscuring the great tree at the heart of the plateau, and his nostrils were full of the stink of ash and burned wood. It was hard to make out distinct shapes, and the sun blazed in his eyes, but Fearless knew Titan was there. He knew it in his blood and bones.

There was a rustle to his left. He halted. A soft *yip* was answered by a staccato howl.

So there were still a few wolves left, the most loyal and dogged of Titan's minions. They'd happily kill him; to kill them first would be no Code-breach. Fearless drew back his lips, exposing his fangs, and gave a low snarl.

Right in front of him, a wolf erupted from the grass, its jaws wide and drooling. Fearless sprang at it, but his teeth only grazed its golden fur before it darted off. He felt a sharp pain in his hind leg, and he spun to catch a wolf this time. His fangs sank into its cheekbone, and he flung it away.

Again a wolf leaped up, almost from beneath his paws; they had burrowed to protect themselves from the smoke, Fearless realized. He dodged the attack and snapped at the wolf's shoulder, but again he felt teeth in his hind leg. These fangs went deeper, and Fearless staggered. Twisting, he lunged and found his tormentor's throat, tearing it out with a quick shake of his head. They were no match.

Panting, he stood motionless, waiting for the next attack. A couple of shadows scuttled at the edge of his vision, but they had seen what had become of two of their pack-mates; they held back, for now.

"Is this how it's going to be, Titan?" he roared, lashing the ground with his paw. "You're going to hide from me, even now? Let your wolves die for nothing, while you cower like a miserable snake?"

"Snakes." The voice that rippled out of the smoke was deep and dark and sinister. "I've eaten snake-spirits. They are with me, fool. All of Bravelands is with me."

"No creature in Bravelands truly stands with a coward," snarled Fearless.

"Ah, you and your precious honor. Just like your stupid father. Look where it got him, Fearless. I'm only sorry I didn't know back then that I could devour his spirit too. Gallant was a strong one, I grant you. But his principles condemned him to death, just as yours will."

Death. The absolute certainty in Titan's voice chilled Fearless's blood, just for an instant. Then he felt a warm certainty of his own. It roiled in his chest, growing and swelling till it was a fire in his heart.

"Today, Death comes for you, Titan."

"Then I will meet Death head-on." A huge-maned silhouette loomed from the drifting smoke. "And I will *eat its heart.*"

Fearless knew he should be terrified, but somehow his fear had drained away. A growl building in his throat, he bounded forward to meet the monstrous lion.

Yet Titan did not move farther. He stood very still. Just as Fearless was within spring-length, he felt a stabbing pain in his cheek, the hot impact of a furred body colliding with his head.

Not a wolf. Too strong for that. Teeth tore at his face, clawing at his eyes. With a roar of frustration, Fearless skidded to a halt, shaking his head violently and lashing at the attacker with a paw.

A lion cub fell away, thudding onto the grass, but swiftly bounced back onto its paws, fangs bared in fury. *Menace!* He had long known she was loyal to her father, and too confident in her abilities. But still, the ferocity of her assault shocked him.

"Stay back, daughter of Titan, if you want to live," roared Fearless. "My fight is with your father!"

She narrowed her flashing eyes. "Then your fight is with me."

Her leap was an astonishing one for a cub of her size. She streaked through the smoky air toward him, but Fearless was ready this time. Rearing back, he struck out with sheathed claws at her snarling head. The cub was tossed back like a bird, crashing to the stunted grass. Menace rolled once, as if to spring up yet again; but the twisting of her body stopped short as she gave a bone-chilling scream of pain. She flopped back, panting and gasping.

Fearless stared at her, tensed to defend himself again if he had to. But Menace struggled to rise, and failed.

Then he saw it: a shard of elephant rib that pierced her haunch, pinning her to the earth. Blood drenched the white bone and dripped down to soak the ground beneath her.

"Get up!" Titan's roar split the silence. "Get up and fight, daughter! Defend your leader and father!"

To Fearless's stomach-churning amazement, she did her best, tearing a deeper wound.

"I'm trying, Father, I'm *trying*. I'll kill him, I'll protect you, I'll—" The cub lurched and kicked, mewling, battling to stand, but the elephant bone held her fast. She was finished, and Fearless couldn't find more than a shred of sympathy.

"Was she your last trick, Titan?" Fearless growled. "It's just you and me now."

Titan's eyes glittered through the smoke trails. "You and me, then, Gallantbrat."

Fearless tensed. He had waited for this moment all his life.

Yet he did not have time to draw a breath before Titan's lightning onrush. There was a spike of fear, a blur of teeth as Titan's jaws stretched wide to seize his throat. But Fearless ducked and they simply collided. The black-maned lion flung

Fearless backward with his sheer weight and speed.

Fearless rolled with the impact, letting himself be driven back even as he bit and snapped and raked with his hind claws at Titan's body. A black throat gaped above his face, blotting out the sky, and he twisted to elude those long yellow teeth, sinking his own fangs into Titan's neck. Most of what he seized was black mane, but his grip kept Titan's teeth from his throat, for a moment at least.

Fearless wrenched himself out from beneath his enemy and sprang for his shoulders. He dug in his claws and hung on, trying to drag Titan down, but the brute's strength was astonishing; Fearless could almost feel the power of him, pulsing violently through his claws. It was like combat with a gigantic buffalo. Except that a buffalo didn't have those fearsome claws.

Grunting, Fearless freed one paw and lashed out at Titan's head, seeking his eyes but managing only a shallow scratch of his muzzle. The older lion twisted, jerked and flung Fearless away. Then, with all the speed of a striking cobra, Titan leaped again, digging his long claws into Fearless's shoulders and pinning *him* to the ground.

The landscape around him became a blur of light and noise as the two lions grappled and fought; blood roared in Fearless's ears, and the dawn light darkened. The struggle had brought them, snapping and twisting and rolling, close to the foot of the eastern cliffs. Merely noticing his surroundings was too much distraction; as Fearless lost his grip on Titan's shoulder, bright hot pain blossomed across his face. Staggering back, he felt hot blood gush into his left eye, and he realized that Titan's claws had ripped down through his eyelid and cheek.

The two lions panted and circled each other. Fearless blinked blood from his eyes, but there was no stopping the stream from his wound; it blinded him again instantly.

Still, the gouges and bites on his body felt unimportant next to the deep agony that spasmed through his side, the side the crocodile had struck with his tail.

Thorn had been right. *I'm hurt. Badly. I can't do this—*

"You're not fighting a lion, do you realize that?" Titan's mocking growl reached him through the thunder of pulsing blood in his ears. "Have you understood it yet, Gallantbrat? You're fighting *Bravelands*. I am more than Titan. I am buffalo, and crocodile, and snake, and cheetah. I am leopard and wild dog and wolf. You think the Great Spirit is powerful? It's *nothing* compared to Titan."

"You are . . . not Bravelands," panted Fearless. "Bravelands and its creatures . . . are everything you are not."

Titan gave a belly-deep laugh of derision. "You've waited your whole life for this, haven't you? Well, it will be worth it, I guarantee that. You will die like all the others, and the spirits of Gallant and Loyal and your mother Swift will look on in despair. Because you will not join them in the stars, after all. You will join *me*. It's a stubborn, courageous heart you have, I'll give you that. Submit now, and I'll tear it from you with little pain."

Another spasm of agony rippled through Fearless, intensified by a dark and heavy despair that threatened to drive him to his knees. He could hardly speak. But he managed one word.

"No."

"Come along, then." Titan danced lightly back on his paws. "Come and hunt down your death."

With that he turned, and, light-footed as an impala, made a springing leap onto a narrow shelf of rock. Fearless gave a groan of frustration and dug his claws into the crumbling rock to scramble up after him. Titan jumped for the next ledge, and the next; Fearless, his chest burning with the effort, hauled himself after him. Here at the edge of the Plain, the dark smoke was thicker, still billowing upward from the smoldering brushwood stacks. It stung Fearless's eyes, making them stream with water that mingled with the blood of his wounds.

Titan is hurt too. Yes, he'd made a few blows count. But the deep scratches and fang punctures did not seem to affect Titan's energy or his arrogant demeanor. And he clearly wasn't half blind as Fearless was.

Out of a blur of smoke and shadow, Titan sprang at him. Fearless reeled back, trading blows with his enemy as he fought to keep his balance on the rocky ledge. As Titan paused, and he staggered, Fearless realized his mouth was filled with blood.

It did not taste of black earth and evil; it wasn't Titan's. Fearless spat it out.

"Nearly there, Gallantbrat, nearly there. Shall I give you your name, out of respect for this last effort of yours? Very well, *Fearless*. There's something I want you to know before I kill you."

Fearless's head reeled. His body was weakening, and his skull felt full of smoke. That taunting voice seemed to come from every direction at once.

"When you're dead, Fearless, I shall pay you an extra tribute. And you'll watch it through my own eyes! I'll find your sister Valor, and her cubs. And that friend of yours, Keen: he deserves my recognition. I'll take their hearts and spirits too, so that they can join you forever. Be grateful, Fearless!"

The new surge of rage seemed to come from nowhere. It was as if the black fires of vengeance had died down abruptly, and new flames of loyalty and love roared up in Fearless's heart. He coiled his muscles.

"You. Will. Not!"

He sprang at Titan, colliding with him head-on. The black-maned lion seemed taken by surprise for once, stumbling backward. Together, they fell from the ledge and crashed to the ground beneath.

Sparks flew up with the impact of their bodies; ash and embers swirled around them both. Tiny thorn-pricks of hot pain burned Fearless's fur, but they seemed like nothing.

Titan, though, was jumping and shaking himself, trying to dislodge the small cinders. His muzzle curling back in hatred, Fearless lunged again.

He knocked Titan clear of the charred fire remnants in another shower of sparks. Grappling together, the two lions rolled and kicked, careering into elephant skeletons. The smallest bones cracked and snapped beneath their struggling bodies, while the larger ones rattled as they scattered.

Titan wriggled free again and staggered between broken elephant ribs. For the first time, he looked disoriented. Fearless jumped after him. Titan swung his haunches around for a counterattack, but he tripped over an exposed thighbone.

He snarled in shock, tumbling clumsily, and Fearless fell on him, snapping wildly.

He could barely see, but he could feel his teeth sink through fur and into flesh, lodging on something hard. *Bone.* Fearless summoned all his strength and ground his jaws together.

Titan's shriek of pain was like the howling of a mass of hyenas. Blinking away the blood, Fearless saw that his fangs had closed tight, in the meat of Titan's foreleg.

Twisting, Titan lashed and scraped with a hind leg, the claws catching Fearless's face again. Fearless knew he could not hold on forever, but he did it for as long as he could, feeling sinew and muscle rip and come apart as Titan squirmed free.

Titan leaped up, his eyes burning with rage. But immediately he swayed and tumbled forward and sideways.

The huge lion clambered to his paws again, but this time he stood on three legs. His mangled foreleg hung useless before him.

Panting, the two lions faced each other. Fearless licked dark blood from his muzzle and blinked.

I'm weak. I'm injured. But now, so is he.

"Remember that day we met, Fearless?"

Fearless growled, low in his throat. "You know I do."

"I killed your father before your eyes. And I watched those eyes of yours. I did." Slowly and meaningfully, Titan licked his bloodied jaws. "You have the same look in them now. Your mother misnamed you, didn't she? Fearless, indeed! You're *terrified*."

"Yes." Fearless gave an exhausted nod. He raised his eyes to Titan's, feeling the Great Spirit's anger pulsate in his blood. "But you feel no fear, even now. You never have. And that, Titan . . . that is why you will die."

Titan began to pace toward him, picking up speed. Fearless rushed to meet him. As the Spirit of Bravelands flooded his body, thundering through his veins, filling his muscles with a power that obliterated all the pain, he leaped high to meet Titan's attack in midair. The sky and earth of Bravelands trembled as Fearless and his enemy collided in a chaos of fang and claw and blood.

CHAPTER TWENTY-TWO

In the wake of the far-off roars and growls, the tumble of rocks, the echoing rattle of bones, and the crash of bodies, the silence that fell was almost unbearable. Rising onto his hind paws, Thorn twisted his fingers together. All he could hear was the frightened breathing of his companions and the thump of his own heart.

He turned to Nut, whose eyes were staring and anxious; he had bitten blood from his lip. Mud trembled. Even Spider stood very still and quiet as his lizard scuttled from one shoulder to the other.

A couple of elephants shifted their feet. Sky's ears flapped forward, and she raised her trunk to scent the burned air. Rock moved closer against her.

From the hushed Fearlesspride, one lion padded forward. Keen bent his head to Thorn.

"Please," he began. "Great Father. Tell me if he lives."

Thorn drew a breath, hesitating. *Do I want to see? What if—*

He shook himself. "All right."

Thorn closed his eyes. Slowly, tentatively, he let his mind reach out across the plateau. Here was an injured wolf: *It's all over for us. Flee, flee, there is nothing for us here. Where is my pack? My pack . . .*

As the thoughts faded to nothing and blackness, Thorn hurriedly slipped out. He crept farther, feeling the stunted grass, the rocks, the smooth bleached bones. The landscape had no mind, no consciousness to inhabit, but still he *felt* it.

But of the two lions, Thorn could find no trace. He reached further, desperate, seeking out Fearless, but he could not locate him.

There was one lion; he felt her, a smaller creature than the ones he sought. With a great sigh, he eased back into his own mind.

"Menace," he said.

She was crawling toward them, dragging herself by her claws. A shard of pale bone jutted from her hind leg, jolting as it dragged behind her. Ignoring the lions, the elephants, and the baboons, she fixed her agonized eyes on the entrance to the Plain and crawled toward it with her horrible encumbrance.

"Menace! Sister!" Ruthless bounded up to her, trying to nuzzle at her face.

He flinched back as she turned her glare on him. "Get away from me. *All of you!*"

"What happened to Fearless?" Thorn ran to Ruthless's side but stopped just out of reach of Menace's bloodied teeth.

"How should I know?" she snarled. "And why would I care?"

They all watched her as she dragged herself painfully slowly through the gate and lurched down the trail.

"Ruthless," began Thorn. "If you want to go after her—"

The young lion shook his head, slowly. "Leave her be," he said softly. "My sister's gone. For good."

"She will die before she reaches the end of the grassland," agreed Nut quietly.

They stared after her until all that remained of Menace's presence was a thin trail of dark, sticky blood. Thorn knew his friend was right. If she didn't perish from her wound, hyenas would finish the job without mercy.

Keen seemed to snap out of a trance. He spun and bounded a few paces back onto the Plain.

"Fearless!" he roared, his hoarse cry echoing from the rock walls. *"Fearless!"*

Thorn hurried to his side and laid a comforting paw on Keen's shoulders. "We'll find him," he murmured. "We'll go together."

Sky walked beside them as Thorn and the young lion made their cautious way across the trampled and torn grass. Sky's ears flapped, and Thorn's too craned for sounds, for groans, for any rustle of a living thing. But there was nothing.

Titan could still be alive, Thorn thought. He could attack at any moment. But if Titan had survived, and Fearless was dead, then hope for Bravelands had died with him.

A curl of pale smoke shifted in a faint breeze, revealing something near the cliffs. Not a boulder, not an elephant skeleton. Creeping forward, Thorn found his pawsteps dragging.

It was the corpse of a lion. Its mane shivered a little in the movement of the air.

Keen came to a stop, and Thorn too halted altogether. If he took one more step, he knew he would fall. Sky strode past them both, her trunk swinging in distress.

Thorn stared at her as she touched the corpse with her trunk, then rolled it over. Sky raised her head and turned it toward him and Keen.

"It's Titan," she called.

Keen gave a hoarse cry of relief and bounded forward, Thorn at his heels. Together they stared down at the torn body of the tyrant.

Titan's eyes were open, but they were blank and drained of life. His foreleg was mutilated, but it was the gaping wound in his throat that had killed him at last. Dark blood, barely clotting, dripped and trickled down to join a vast wet stain of it beneath his head and black mane. Flies already buzzed around his corpse.

Thorn shuddered, torn by a mixture of horror and utter relief. Keen, though, showed no further interest in the lifeless corpse. He sprang away at speed.

"Fearless!" he cried.

Thorn gasped. Keen was racing toward another mounded shape in the grass, farther away in the shadow of the cliff.

Together, Thorn and Sky turned their backs on Titan and bolted after Keen.

"Is he—" Thorn stumbled to a halt at Keen's side.

"He's alive," croaked Keen.

Fearless's flanks twitched, feebly, with shallow breaths. Thorn put his paws over his mouth to stifle a cry of distress. Blood coated his friend's fur in great patches; where the fur was visible, it was spotted with smaller scorch marks. One of his eyes was stuck shut, clotted with more dark blood from a ragged gash on his forehead. A flap of skin had been ripped from his cheek and muzzle, exposing his fangs. His tail was severed almost through, and clumps of hair had been torn from his mane. They swirled and blew across the grass in the rising breeze.

Sky sucked in a breath. She reached out her quivering trunk and caressed his face with its tip. Keen licked gently at his friend's torn muzzle.

Fearless's eyelid flickered, and his good eye swiveled to find Keen.

"Fearless," Keen whispered. "Fearless, you're going to be fine. Stand up. Please, stand up."

"It's all right, Keen." The whisper was barely audible.

"No, it's not all right." Keen licked his ear urgently, then pressed his face to his friend's. "You have to get up. You can rest later. I know it hurts, but—"

"It doesn't hurt," rasped Fearless. "Not at all. Not anymore."

"Fearless." Keen's mewl of distress was almost unbearable; Thorn wanted to put his paws over his ears, but he mustn't. He could feel the hot grief already, building under his breastbone, ready to swell and swallow him up.

"Keen, don't be sad. Thorn. Sky. I'm . . . glad to see you again."

Thorn crouched by his head. He stroked Fearless's mane, over and over again. "You fulfilled your oath, Fearless," he croaked. "Titan's gone. You did it."

Keen seemed to give up at last. He lay down close against Fearless, pressing his head to his friend's. He closed his eyes, giving a shuddering breath, and lay very still.

Thorn, too, closed his eyes. At last he found what he'd been searching for, and he realized suddenly why he hadn't been able to locate it before. He'd been searching for a mind full of vengeance and bitterness and regret, and most of all anger.

But Fearless was none of those things. He was calm, and he'd told his friends the truth: it didn't hurt. The pain was like a distant memory. He had done everything he was supposed to do, and that was a restful feeling. He didn't remember when he'd felt such peace: a long time ago, perhaps when he'd curled against his mother as a cub?

Thorn reeled, lost in a memory not his own, but falling into it was not unsettling: it was calm, a deep well of peace. A lioness came padding to his side; her eyes, once scarred and blinded, were clear and bright. She nuzzled his wounded cheek, a gentle rumble of happiness in her throat.

"Well done, my Swiftcub. My Fearless. It's time to sleep now." Swift's tongue came out to smooth his rumpled ear fur. "It's been a long day."

"Yes, Mother," he murmured.

"Your father is proud." She smiled, pressing her muzzle against his. "Both of them are."

Thorn-Fearless twisted his head to find them. His fathers stood a little way away, side by side, watching him. Gallant grunted softly in greeting. Loyal gave Fearless a nod of pride. Then they both began to turn away.

Wait for me. . . .

The two great lions paused, looking back at him. He felt his mother's tongue caress his cheek again.

"Of course they're waiting, Fearless. This time, you can go with them."

He could. Of course he could. The realization was like a dawn ray. It wasn't as if he was in pain now. Rising swiftly to his paws, free of pain, he shook out his magnificent mane.

Fearless pressed his face to his mother's, full of gratitude and love. She watched him fondly as he turned and set out on eager paws after Loyal and Gallant. Because he could keep up with them, now. Even though they were racing up thin air toward the stars, he could follow. He was going with them at last—

Thorn pulled free with a gasping sob.

"Thorn?" Keen's head jerked up.

Thorn didn't reply. He felt Sky's trunk stroke his shoulder as he moved forward to place a paw against Fearless's wounded chest.

No movement. No beat of a fierce and courageous heart. Squeezing his eyes tight shut, Thorn heard Keen's tormented roar of misery.

Fearless was dead.

When he blinked his eyes open, the sky had darkened. Wasn't it morning, then? Had the whole day passed as they mourned their friend?

Then Thorn realized what it was. Sky raised her head, too, and gazed at the vast flock of vultures that swept over the Plain.

Thorn felt a flash of pointless resentment. *Not yet, not yet! Please, Windrider . . .*

But she and her flock did not settle near Fearless's body. They flew down to Titan, hopping and flapping till they had gathered in a black mass of wings around his corpse. As Thorn, Keen, and Sky stared, Windrider herself hopped forward to the thing that lay at the heart of their circle: the torn body of the lion.

She sank her long beak into the ragged wound on Titan's throat, tugging free a strip of flesh. Throwing back her head, she gulped it down as her flock watched in silence.

Her head swiveled, and her black eyes met Thorn's.

"The death is a good one," she croaked in Skytongue. "Indeed, the best."

He nodded to acknowledge her verdict. His voice trembling, he told her: "I will tell all the animals of Bravelands."

Windrider turned back to her flock; not one of them had moved. Even now, they didn't tear into Titan's carcass, and

Thorn frowned in puzzlement. They seemed to be watching Windrider, pausing for further commands.

"Wait," was all she said.

Something stirred above Titan's body: a ripple in the air. It trembled, and Thorn felt a vibration passing through him, as if thunder had cracked the sky nearby.

The smoke . . .

Trails and traces of it still lingered, but Thorn was sure the breeze and the early light were playing tricks on his eyes. The smoke coiled and parted and coalesced again, outlining the forms of . . . animals?

Yes, they were animals. A cheetah made of smoke and air bounded free of Titan's body, sprinting toward the arc of the sky. On her heels came two buffalo, snorting puffs of white breath as substantial as they were themselves. They too thundered skyward.

And suddenly misty shapes were pouring from the lion's lifeless corpse, a Great Herd made of shifting smoke. Thorn gaped, his heart pounding against his ribs. A young elephant, capering playfully as impalas and a rhino bounded past him. A splendid lion, his eyes glowing with the joy of freedom. A crocodile swam upward, as sleek and fast as if it were in unseen water. Zebras, a serval cat, and a leopard; a gerenuk, another cheetah; a cluster of warthogs who looked more cheerful than any Thorn had seen in life.

The vultures simply observed it all, still and silent. On they came, the spirits Titan had devoured: ostriches, a hippo, rats and ground squirrels and meerkats. The other animals watched, enrapt as Thorn.

"They're free," said Sky, her voice choked. "They're going to the stars, as they were always meant to."

"Fearless . . ." Keen cleared his throat and tried to say the name again. "Will—will Fearless go there?"

"He already has." Thorn reached out a paw to touch the young lion's mane, but he could not avert his eyes to look at him. He was searching the mist-formed host, the dead of Bravelands, hunting desperately for a familiar beautiful shape, the stump of a lost tail. *She must be with them. She'll go to the stars now. Even if I don't see her, I know she's there.*

High above them, the mist was dissipating, the shapes lost as smoke and spirits melted into the high streaks of cloud. Thorn blinked hard.

"Was she there? Was Berry with them?" he asked desperately.

"I didn't see her," said Sky gently. "But she was there. Be sure of that, Thorn."

The vultures at last seemed ready to feast. They spread their wings, hopped into better positions, glanced hopefully at Windrider. She dipped her head.

But before they could tear into Titan's carcass, there was a tremble of approaching feet. Boulder trotted up in a cloud of ash and dust, swinging his trunk irritably at the vultures, who squawked in offense. Even Windrider looked unsettled and cross.

"Not here," he rumbled. He curled his long trunk around Titan's hind leg and dragged him toward the plateau entrance. "Rot-eaters, you can feast outside."

Thorn watched Boulder haul the tattered corpse to the entrance and fling it out onto the trail. The vultures rose in a flapping, squawking mass, then settled again beyond the boundary wall.

And that is the last I want to think about Titan. Thorn turned anxiously to Sky. "What about Fearless? Boulder won't—"

"No," Sky reassured him. "No elephant will ever disrespect Fearless's remains. I promise you, Thorn, and Keen. He will rest here, on the Plain of Our Ancestors, until the sun touches his bones."

"What?" Thorn took a sharp breath. "You mean it, Sky?"

"Of course I mean it. Fearless will always live in our memories."

She turned to caress Keen's bowed head, then touched Thorn's face gently with her trunk-tip.

"So long as there are elephants, Fearless will have our respect and gratitude. His body will rest here with our blessing." She smiled. "But his spirit will hunt among the stars."

CHAPTER TWENTY-THREE

"Oh, don't fuss, Blossom," complained *Thorn,* tugging his paw away from the Goodleaf. "It's nothing serious."

The shadows of Dawntrees were a cool respite after the blazing heat of the high Plain of Our Ancestors. Baboons moved busily through the trees and bushes, repairing nests, collecting fruit, nursing infants. It all felt so beautifully *normal*, thought Sky, toying with a mango as she watched Thorn grouse at the Goodleaf.

"Great Father, you must rest and let me heal you." Blossom's dark eyes twinkled. "You are important to all of us, and it's my job to keep you in good health. Isn't that right, Sky Strider?" She smiled up at Sky, then scowled at the bite marks and scratches on Thorn's chest, pressing more chewed leaves to them. "Ugh. The Crown Guard were vicious. And Menace might have been a small lion, but she was still a *lion*."

"Blossom's right, Thorn," Sky agreed, amused. "Even a Great Father should behave himself for the Goodleaves."

"You'll be fine, Thorn," added Blossom, patting his arm. "But you need to rest." She glanced up at the branch of the kigelia tree above them. "What do you think, little Green-shoot? Would you like to become a Goodleaf when you're older?"

Snuggled against his new mother, Scratcher, Greenshoot peered down in fascination. Scratcher stroked his little head gently. The old baboon still looked awed and astonished by her good fortune and her new baby. *If there's one good choice Creeper made*, thought Sky, *it was this one.*

Thorn sighed, submitting at last to the Goodleaf's atten-tion. Maybe, thought Sky, they should just have let him complain and protest. Now that he was silent, Thorn's eyes became distant and sad. He was still thinking about Fear-less, she knew. It was hardly surprising. Reaching out with her trunk, she nuzzled his shoulder.

He sighed again and tipped his head back to stare up into the branches. "This tree," he murmured. "You know it's the very one where Stinger first found Fearless?"

"I'm not sure I did know that," said Sky.

"His 'Cub of the Stars.'" Thorn smiled sadly. "And now Fearless has gone back there."

"I know how much you miss him," she said softly. "I do, too."

"I don't think I'll ever stop missing him." Thorn's head drooped. "I can't imagine life in Bravelands without him."

Sky felt the weight of the grief as it churned again in her chest. "I know," she whispered. "But Fearless wouldn't want us to think that way, I'm sure of it. He died to defend Bravelands, and our lives here. He'd want us to enjoy those lives, Thorn— he bought them so dearly. And his legacy—that's still with us. Fearlesspride follows the Great Spirit now."

"Yes." Thorn nodded. "And I'll tell his story till I go and join him, Sky." He gave her a rueful twist of his muzzle.

Sky dipped her head to curl her trunk around his shoulders. "It's time for me to leave, Thorn. I wanted to see you and Dawntrees, but this is good-bye for now."

"I knew this was coming." He patted her trunk. "Go well, Sky. Be with your family."

"May the Great Spirit watch over you, Thorn, and all your troop. I know it will."

She turned and strode away more swiftly than she'd meant to; it was so hard to walk away from Thorn, but what she'd told him was true: it was time. Long past time.

Rock waited for her at the border of the forest, his dark hide mottled by sunlight. He raised his trunk in greeting, spreading his ears as she walked toward him. Her heart soared, as it always did at the sight of him; his green eyes were full of warmth . . . and a touch of regret.

"We go our separate ways now, Sky."

"Yes." She butted her head gently against his. "I wish I could stay with you forever, Rock. I'll miss you."

"It's not the elephant way," he murmured.

"I know. I accept that, now." She gave a deep sigh. "It's been

long, long seasons since I followed the customs. Since Great
Mother died, I've picked my own path."

"That was right and good," Rock assured her. "You were
true to yourself—true to Bravelands and the Great Spirit.
Great Mother would be so proud of you."

Inside, Sky felt a warm thrill. She *had* done the right thing,
however badly it conflicted with the traditions of her kind.

Rock twined his trunk with hers. "It won't be as long as it
seems," he whispered. "I'll see you again soon, Sky. On the
Plain of Hearts."

Keeping her eyes fixed on that deep green gaze, Sky drew
slowly away. Her trunk slid through his, feeling the warmth
of Rock's touch till the last possible moment until they broke
contact.

Then she backed away another step, turned, and walked
away across the grassland. Comet and the other females and
calves waited there in the hazy sunlight, their ears flapping
eagerly, their trunks raised in welcome.

"Welcome, Sky." Comet blew an affectionate breath at her
shoulder.

"Sky!" blared Horizon. "I'm glad to have you on the trek."

One by one, the females fell into file behind Comet, with
calls of greeting to Sky and fleeting touches as they passed
her. They nudged and encouraged the calves, who trotted by
with wondering glances at Sky. One tiny calf stared so long,
she almost tripped over her own feet. Laughing, her mother
steadied her with her trunk.

"Yes, Acacia. That *is* the famous Sky Strider!"

Filled with renewed certainty, Sky joined the column beside her aunts and cousins. *They are my family. I belong now.* She was an ordinary elephant at last, walking with the female herd, caring for the youngsters, and obeying her matriarch. It felt right. It felt *good.* And in only a season, Rock would come to meet her on the Plain of Hearts.

"How does it feel, Sky?" murmured Horizon at her side.

She smiled. "Isn't it much more peaceful to be normal again?"

About to answer, Sky saw two lithe shadows dart between her feet. She hesitated, raising a foot to clear the way of the young cheetahs, Nimble and Lively.

"We're going with the elephants!" chirped Nimble.

"Yay!" cried Lively. "We're staying with Sky!"

The pair of them tumbled, rolled, and jumped up to dart forward through the tramping legs of the herd. Horizon burst out laughing, and Sky chuckled with her.

"Much more peaceful," she told Horizon mischievously. "But maybe not *entirely* normal!"

EPILOGUE

Five years later

Far below Windrider, the golden plains of Bravelands shimmered in the sun's heat. The air currents were warm on her black wings, the sky clear almost to the horizon, but she could see clouds building beyond it, towering masses of gray that must be unseen by the animals below. The rains were coming, and they would be good this season: Bravelands would be lush and green once more, and the herds would thrive; that meant in turn that the predators and the rot-eaters would fare just as well.

Angling her wings, she peered down harder, curious. On the yellow grassland by a winding silver river, two prides of lions faced each other down. The leaders stood face-to-face. A territorial dispute, she guessed. Perhaps that younger lion had chosen to challenge the larger one for this fine and open stretch of the savannah?

That was a misjudgment on his part, she thought. The young male had a fine mane, but even from this height, Windrider could see that he was clearly outmatched by the powerful older lion; this would not end well for him. Had the Great Spirit not given the youngster its guidance? Such foolishness would always end in a humiliating beating.

But her role was only to watch. Windrider circled lower, intrigued.

The youngster had nerve, she gave him that. He was prowling forward, judging his spring, baring his fangs in challenge. She felt a tug of amusement. He would learn his lesson—and swiftly, judging by the coiling muscles of his golden-maned opponent.

The challenger leaped, colliding in midair with his opponent. The two fell back to the ground, legs flailing, as they rolled and tussled in a cloud of pale dust.

Strange that the older lion seemed to be holding back; it wasn't like such a magnificent male to show mercy to a challenger. Fascinated, Windrider swooped even lower.

Not a drop of blood had been spilled. The lions snapped and bit and pummeled each other, but fangs did not sink into flesh, and the blows were delivered with claws sheathed. *Ah*, she thought, *it's only a play-fight. They are friends.*

As they tired at last, the two lions flopped apart, panting. The dust settled around them; Windrider glided down to the earth at a decent distance. She knew them now: that pale mane on the younger one, the rangy frame of his senior. Ruthless Ruthlesspride and Keen Keenpride. Keen rolled over happily, paddling his long legs, and Ruthless butted his cheek and nuzzled him.

Windrider folded her wings and hunched her shoulders, watching. Each of the lions had a fine pride, with many lionesses and healthy-looking cubs. Her eyes had seen much in her long life; her heart was old and worn and tough, but still it warmed at the sight.

Through her talons, she felt the ground tremble. Windrider glanced to the side. A baby elephant was careering toward her: one moment shying away, then, overcome with curiosity, trotting closer. The elephant flapped her baby ears, then raised her trunk and blew a high-pitched trumpet of excitement. Windrider winced at the racket and narrowed her eyes, and the baby drummed her front feet as if to scare her.

Windrider held her ground. The little elephant might be many times her size, but it had been many, many years since she had been scared by a baby. She opened her beak, spread her wings, and squawked. The young elephant gave a startled squeal of fright and twisted her head to look for her mother.

A female elephant approached, looking unconcerned. "What are you up to, Moonbeam? Trying to scare a vulture?" She laughed.

"It's trying to scare *me*," said Moonbeam indignantly.

The mother laughed again. "Oh, I'm sure that isn't even possible." She caressed her baby's head with her trunk. "Is it?"

"No way!" squealed Moonbeam, capering away.

Windrider's gaze met the young mother's. *How happy Sky*

looks, she thought. She had grown into a fine elephant, her tusks long and creamy, and there was such a deep contentment in her eyes.

Windrider stretched her wings, hopped, and lurched skyward once again. Below, Sky was following her little calf back across the grassland to join the female herd that browsed in a cluster of acacias. *So Comet is still their matriarch*, thought Windrider, gazing at the magnificent old elephant who watched over the herd. *But I don't doubt Sky will take on that responsibility, one day.*

She climbed a little higher, angling her broad wings. The sunlit expanse of Bravelands rushed beneath her, plain and river and kopje. A ravine's shadow opened in the ground below, and she swooped down once more, finding Thorn crouched in the branches of a gnarled mango tree. Slowing her flight, she flapped down and perched close to him.

Thorn blinked his eyes open. "Thank you, Windrider, for letting me see through your eyes." He smiled at her. "All is well in Bravelands, then. And Sky looks so happy. Her baby is beautiful."

She dipped her head to him and took off without a word. He didn't mind that. They had known each other so long now, he rarely needed to hear the old bird's Skytongue.

He watched her as she circled up and up on the air currents, till she was no more than a black dot in the arc of the sky. The dazzle stung his eyes, so he turned back to the ground beneath the old tree, where Mud was tossing his stones.

His small friend's fur was grizzled now, flecked with gray, but then so was Thorn's. "What do the stones say, Mud?" he called.

Mud twisted to grin up at him. "Nothing alarming, Great Father. All is well. How does Bravelands look from above?"

"Just as the stones tell you, old friend." Thorn smiled. "The long peace continues, thank the Great Spirit."

"Hey, you two!" Nut bounded across the stones toward the mango tree. His movements were not as lithe and quick as they'd once been, but his scarred old face had a look of wisdom and nobility. It was a good trade, thought Thorn.

"The troop is all going to watch the first Three Feats challenge," Nut went on, "back at Tall Trees, before sunset. You want to come?"

"I'll watch." Mud gathered up his stones. "What about you, Thorn?"

"I'll follow shortly," Thorn called down.

"Don't be long," growled Nut. "These youngsters need a *lot* of advice. Useless bunch, they are. Spider's already trying to explain to them about eagle eggs, but will they listen? Not one of them would have made Middleleaf back in our day. Hmph!"

Thorn watched his two friends go with an inward smile. When the sound of their pawsteps had faded over the edge of the ravine, he began to clamber down through the twisted branches, tugging a ripe mango from one as he went. He cupped it carefully in one paw. The gully was a bad place for a mango tree to seed, but this one had survived, and it always managed to produce a few fruits in its season. Funnily enough, though the tree's crop was small, its fruits were always especially big and sweet, as if to compensate for its harsh environment.

Jumping down, Thorn loped toward the old acacia farther up the slope. Placing his free paw against it, he pressed his forehead to the rough bark. How many seasons had it been now since he'd met Berry in the shade of these branches? Yet if he closed his eyes, it was as if he could still feel her presence. As if he would blink them open and see her there, waiting for him with glowing, excited eyes, close enough to touch her golden fur. *Close enough to embrace her . . .*

He scrambled up to the acacia's lowest branch. There was a cleft in it; gently he placed the mango there, lodging it securely but carefully so that he wouldn't bruise or break its red-gold skin. He leaned back against the trunk, gazing up toward the ravine's rim. Beyond it lay Bravelands, at peace. It was a good thought.

"I wish you could be here, Berry," he said aloud. "You'd be so happy. We both would, at last."

He wouldn't close his eyes, not this time. It hurt his heart too much when he opened them again to find her nearness was an illusion. Instead Thorn focused on the pale rocks where they'd hunted together for centipedes, on the blades of yellow grass stirred by the warm breeze at the ravine's edge. It was so still here, so beautiful.

The breeze faded. A soft paw touched his. A head rested warm against his shoulder, and aching longing flooded his heart.

No, he must not turn to look; must not break the spell.

Better just to sit here, in the calmness of the Bravelands afternoon, until the dusk turned the sky to lilac.